HANDLING SUSANNAH

Mail-Order Grooms, Book 1

AMELIA SMARTS

Published by Amelia Smarts
ameliasmarts.com

Smarts, Amelia
Handling Susannah

Cover Design by germancreative
Images by The Killion Group, Inc.

ISBN: 9781548626075

Chapter One

Texas, 1892

Adam yearned to hold a sweet, innocent woman in his arms. He wanted to hear her sighs as he touched and kissed her. He wanted to scrape his fingers through silky locks of hair and nibble on that part of her body where her delicate neck curved into shoulder. A deep breath of feminine scent would be a welcome change from the decidedly male smells around him—cows, sweat, and leather. His cock tightened his denims, and he groaned. His aching manhood would find no home between a woman's legs in the foreseeable future, unless he decided to visit one of the painted ladies in town. He didn't want that. The pleasure he was looking for would only come from teaching an unspoiled woman about the joys of carnal love.

He untied the bandana from around his neck and mopped his face with the damp cotton. The scorching mid-June climate in northwest Texas was plenty hot enough without his bawdy daydream to fuel the fire of lust burning within him. He nudged his mare into a faster walk. It was late afternoon and he was determined to check the entire perimeter of his ranch before calling it a day and returning to his lonely cabin and empty bed.

He shushed the voice inside his head telling him his efforts to maintain the ranch were useless. His failing business was months, if not weeks away from bankruptcy. Soon he would be chased off the very land his father had left him.

His grasslands had been taken over by sheep, driven by opportunistic, thieving sheepherders. Though Adam had put up a valiant fight over the last year, the boundaries depicted in the deed to his land were too vague to act as evidence that all the land was actually his. He attended court hearings in between training horses, branding cattle, and overseeing his hands. He hunted down witnesses who knew his pa and how he'd traveled from St. Louis to Amarillo to settle the land along with other old-timers.

But each day in court ended in more bad news, with Adam unable to prove he owned the land. His poor father would be rolling over in his grave if he knew his only living son was about to lose the ranch he'd worked so hard to acquire and build from scratch.

Adam would've liked to strangle the lawyer who helped his father draw up the will and deed, but that man was long gone with the money his father had paid him. It made Adam angry and intolerant in a big way toward dishonest men. It was because of a dishonest lawyer, dishonest herders, and an incompetent system that he was about to lose everything. Still, until he'd actually lost the ranch, he would take care of business. He would care for the cattle and horses, fix the fences, and try to sell his stock at a profit, just as he had always done. Adam's pa had said more than once he was stubborn as a mule. That wasn't always a good quality, but it did make Adam someone who did not quit.

As he walked his horse beside the old wooden fence, he gritted his teeth with anger at what lay ahead. Sheep were grazing among his cattle on his last fertile meadow. His anger and dismay grew the closer he rode to the sheep, for as he neared, he saw that the earth beneath the animals was ruined. Grass wouldn't grow in this part of his range for months, which meant that most of his cattle would have to be sold off for a loss. Yes, he was definitely within weeks of losing everything.

Adam removed the horsewhip attached to his hip, uncoiled it with a flick of his wrist, and cracked it in the air. It took a solid hour of hard riding and frustration, but eventually he corralled the sheep back to where they belonged on the other side of the fence.

Swinging down from his horse, he observed the horizontal slats of wood and cursed. It was just as he suspected. The break was manmade, since the jagged edges of the wood were clean and without rot, broken in pieces against the grain. With anger acting as his main source of energy, Adam repaired the fence as best he could, using nails and a hammer he carried in his saddlebag for that very purpose. With how things had been going, the offending herder would likely break the fence again within a week. Adam would make efforts to be around to lambast the son-of-a-bitch next time.

Adam trotted his mare to town. He might as well report the theft to the marshal, though he knew it would do little good, with the marshal being just shy of useless. The best Adam could hope for was that the marshal would temporarily halt the progression of sheepherders overtaking him in order to give him a chance to slaughter or sell his herd before they starved.

When he reached the town's center, he tethered his mare loosely to the hitching post outside of the marshal's office. She drank from the trough of clean water next to it. Adam dunked his bandana, wrung it out, and mopped his face, trying to cool down. Between his unbidden lust and his anger, Adam burned as hot as an untamed prairie fire.

He strode through the front door of the marshal's office to an empty room, dirtying the hardwood floor with his dusty boots. "Perfect," he muttered. He either had to wait for the marshal to return or go out searching for him. Adam opted for the former because his body was aching and weary from the labor of the day. He sat on a straight-backed wooden chair and picked up the newspaper on the table next to it. It was a paper from New York, found quite often in the jailhouse. Adam guessed the marshal subscribed to it in order to provide a glimpse into some of the more civilized happenings around the country.

Texas was in the news. Inside were stories about ranchers and sheepherders scrapping over grasslands. The upcoming election made the front page, but Adam had never been all that interested in politics. Bored, he read the personals, which generally provided him with some amusement. The paper was always full of mail-order bride requests written by men with the same longing for a woman that Adam felt.

He'd never more than briefly considered running one of his own ads for a woman, mostly because he couldn't afford one. Men often lied in the listings about their financial situation, but Adam wouldn't do that. Besides offending his sense of right and wrong, he didn't see the point of being deceptive, even if the lies worked and he managed to wrangle himself a wife. When she figured out his dirt-poor status, she would be disappointed, and he'd rather eat dust every day for supper than disappoint a woman 'til death did them part.

Adam felt his eyebrows head north when he came across a very unusual advertisement. It appeared he was not the only person to find it interesting, as it had been circled several times with some force behind the pencil. Narrowing his eyes, he read the short paragraph for the second time to make sure he wasn't misunderstanding it somehow.

Woman, 22, seeks husband age 22 to 35 with experience ranching. Must be strong and dependable. Woman is heir to profitable cattle ranch, needs husband to take possession of deed and run business. Those interested, write to Susannah Smith of Virginia City, Nevada.

Adam guffawed out loud, hardly believing a woman would be so foolish as to write such a thing. She would receive hundreds of responses. How would she ever decide which man would be suitable? And why couldn't she find a suitor within her own town? He doubted there was a shortage of lonely cowboys in Virginia City.

He had many more questions, and he grew more curious the longer he stared at the paper. He reckoned he was as suitable a candidate as any other. He'd learned how to swing a lasso when he was barely knee-high to his pa, and he'd have to take a guess about which he'd learned to do first—walk or ride a horse. Then there were the cattle. He had a good eye for choosing bulls and cows. He knew how to breed them and how to ensure they were properly grazed. Sure, his ranch was failing, but that was entirely outside of his control.

Worry for this young woman who'd put herself out in the world so boldly intermingled with his curiosity. She had made herself a target for liars and thieves. The prospect of suddenly owning a readymade cattle ranch would be mighty tempting to any man, including himself.

Surely something was wrong, though. The woman was likely ugly as sin. He could live with that, he supposed, if she was agreeable and obedient, of upstanding character, and a good cook.

Adam decided not to wait for the marshal and instead see about sending a message to Miss Susannah Smith. It couldn't hurt anything but his pride if she didn't accept him, since he had nothing else to lose. With this in mind, he walked to the telegraph station, intent on sending Miss Smith a telegram using a quarter he otherwise would have spent on grain. The clerk, a portly man in his grizzled years, handed him a small piece of paper and a pencil, which Adam twirled in his fingers for a while, considering how to phrase a response. He had only one shot, and he needed to get it right. Finally, he came to a decision about how to begin the correspondence:

Regarding your request for a mail-order groom…

He and the telegraph clerk engaged in moment of raucous laughter. Though the woman hadn't defined it as such, a mail-ordered groom was exactly what she was requesting, and Adam thought a little levity would be the best approach in his communication with her. The rest of the telegram discussed matters of importance.

…I am a strong 30-year-old rancher of sound mind, good character, and decent appearance interested in your unique request for both a husband and a man to run your business. Please respond to Adam Harrington of Amarillo, Texas.

It wasn't a bad-sounding note, but he imagined that the woman had already received many telegrams that read much the same, and she would have no way to know he was telling the truth. An irrational desire to throttle the other men who would respond struck him. He knew many would inflate their experience or reduce their age.

Still, he couldn't help but be a little excited as he rode home. For the first time in a long while, he felt a bit of hope for the future. If nothing else, the telegram was his first step in moving on. It was his first step in recognition of the fact that he was about to lose his ranch and it was time start a new life.

* * *

When the response from Susannah Smith came, Adam had all but forgotten the strange ad in the paper, for his days were occupied with selling off his cattle and the furniture in his cabin. He needed to get some cash in his billfold and head west where cattlemen were needed.

The clerk's young boy rode out to his ranch at a gallop to deliver the message. After the boy hopped off the horse and the cloud of dust settled, he panted, "You got a letter from Virginia City today, Mr. Harrington!" A lopsided grin appeared on his freckled face as he held out the envelope with the message inside.

"Thanks, son." Adam fished in his pocket for a penny and found one. Dropping it into the boy's hand, he said, "Tell your pa I'm mighty grateful he had you deliver it straight away."

"It's no trouble, Mr. Harrington. Aren't you gonna open it?" Wide, curious eyes studied the missive in Adam's hand.

Adam felt a dull ache in his chest, as he often did when he dealt with children. They reminded him of his brother and sister, who had died in childhood. His brother, a year older than he, had broken his neck falling from the barn's loft. His sister, two years younger, had died from diphtheria. As a result of these tragedies, Adam had no desire to have children of his own. It seemed like an awful lot of responsibility with too much room for error, and witnessing his parents' heartbreak had broken Adam's heart as well.

It was just as well that he didn't want children, since having a wife had always been little more than a notion. He waved the boy away. "Yes, I'm gonna open it, just as soon as you mosey on back to town, Jimmy."

The boy made no move to leave and continued to look at him with an expectant expression.

"Don't be nosy, young man. It doesn't suit you," Adam admonished with a frown. He reckoned that the boy's father had told him about the possible contents of the letter. "Go on, get yourself gaited," Adam said, tossing his head in the direction of town. "And no galloping. You walk that horse back to town sensible-like, or I'll be having a word with your pa."

The boy's shoulders slumped a bit. "All right, Mr. Harrington," he mumbled. "I'll be seein' you then."

Adam watched Jimmy and his horse disappear over a rolling hill in the distance and then looked at the letter in his hand. He was hesitant to open it. His hopes had just risen higher than a Ponderosa pine. If the message in the envelope was anything but positive, his fall back to earth would be about as enjoyable as getting bucked off a bronco.

Finally, he gritted his teeth, hooked his thumb under the flap, and ripped the envelope open. What he pulled out first was a photograph of a young woman. His breath hitched. Staring back at him was quite possibly the most beautiful woman he'd ever laid eyes on, in picture or in person. Her hair was light and shining. She had dancing, mischievous eyes, and her pretty, plump lips quirked up ever-so-slightly in a smile that caused blood to travel straight to his loins. She held her slender shoulders very straight, boosting voluptuous breasts, the size of which were not disguised despite being fully and modestly covered by a calico bodice.

Adam realized he was holding his breath and let it out, silently scolding himself for the wicked thoughts running through his mind. Oh, the things he would like to do to her. He imagined that she was quite innocent about bedroom activities, for she was ladylike in appearance. It would be his pleasure and hers to teach her a thing or two. A beautiful, innocent woman would make a fine wife indeed.

He set the photograph aside and pulled out the letter, which he unfolded slowly, his heart thumping painfully against his chest.

Mr. Harrington, provided that you were honest in your correspondence, I accept your offer of marriage and placement as overseer of my ranch. Please take the stagecoach west at your earliest convenience. The ranch needs immediate attention. Yours, Miss Susannah Smith

Adam could hardly believe what he had just read. How had he gotten so lucky? Not only was he about to be in possession of a new ranch, his intended was so beautiful it felt sinful just looking at her picture.

Then his rational faculties kicked in and Adam worried that something wasn't quite right. The whole situation seemed too good to be true. What if it was some kind of ruse? He tried to imagine ways he could be bamboozled in this situation, but he couldn't think of what motivation the woman would have for lying. Surely she understood that if anything she said wasn't true, it would take him no longer than an hour or two upon arrival to discover it.

He studied the photograph once again, this time attempting to ignore her perfect skin and the swell of her breasts. He searched her face for deceit. He couldn't find any. Neither could he find truth, though, so her photograph was of little use in ascertaining her character. Of course, it couldn't be said that he was a good judge of character when it came to looks. The lawyer who'd helped his father draw up the useless deed had the most honest face Adam had ever seen.

"You belong in the looney bin," he muttered to himself more than once over the next few days, as he sold off and packed up his earthly belongings.

With one final look at his lost ranch, Adam left for Virginia City with high hopes and buried fears.

Chapter Two

Three weeks later

Susannah woke up early, which was unusual, since she generally slept in until well after dawn. She felt scared, so sleep wasn't coming easy as of late.

Am I about to make the biggest mistake of my life? she wondered for the thousandth time. That would really be something, considering the mountain of mistakes she'd already made in her twenty-two years.

As she combed her blonde hair with an engraved oak hairbrush that had belonged to her long-deceased mother, she comforted herself with the knowledge that, really, sending away for a husband had been her only sane choice. In Virginia City, she had a reputation for being a loose woman, so the men who had tried to court her were bottom of the barrel, to put it nicely. She had no problem attracting drunks, sluggards, and bunko artists, but she needed a hardworking rancher for a husband, one who would follow her orders.

A man who was both capable of ranching and docile enough to follow directions was not easy to find. If a man was capable, he tended to be stubborn, and if a man was docile, he tended to be unqualified. She could not abide either. A hardheaded husband would only make her life miserable, for he would not heed her wishes. A bad worker would lead her to financial ruin.

Susannah opened the door to the hallway. She heard a loud *pop* and quickly stepped back before the heavy wood hit her toe. *Another broken door*, she grumbled to herself as her heart pounded from the near-injury to her person. She examined the side of it and noticed that one of the hinges had come free, meaning she would have to lift the door in order to close it. She decided to open it instead and leave it that way until it was fixed.

A small thrill of hope and happiness shot through her. Soon she would be married, and a man's strength was what she needed. She would instruct him to fix the bedroom door. She would also tell him to fix the broken padlocks on the barn, the floorboards with holes that were hazardous when stepped on, the window that had caked mud where glass should be, the leaking roof of the chicken coop, and the fence around the perimeter of the ranch.

Her new husband would be busy, that was for certain, but it was a fair bargain. After all, he would acquire a fertile plot of ground, four hundred head of cattle, twenty chickens, twelve horses, a house, and a barn.

And he would acquire her and her son too, of course. A tremor went through her as it did every time she thought about having to explain the existence of her son to her future husband.

Susannah retrieved a pan from the doorless cupboard. She was a terrible cook, something her new husband wouldn't discover until after he married her—thank goodness. She hadn't had a mother growing up, and though the ranch foreman's wife had taught her the basics, Susannah found cooking boring and she lacked creativity when it came to preparing meals.

Her father had kept in his employ a cook and a maid who would ride out to their cabin a few times a week, but both had quit after he died because Susannah failed to pay them in a timely manner. Making sense of bills was extremely difficult for her even now, eleven months after his death, and she often wished her pa had taught her more about responsibility, rather than spoiling her as he had. She learned the hard way that getting what she wanted, immediately and without trying very hard, could lead to unimaginable heartache further on down the road. As a child, instant gratification had meant candy and toys, which were harmless enough. But as a young woman, that had transformed into a need for instant sex and love. She'd pursued both with reckless abandon, and she lived with the consequences of that every day.

Susannah placed the pan on the oven and fired up the logs in the pit, then plopped a dollop of butter and six strips of bacon into the pan. Soon the cabin was filled with the heavenly scent of fried bacon. The loud sizzling drowned out some of the scary thoughts running through her head.

She smiled at five-year-old Caleb as he stumbled in the direction of food, rubbing his eyes. "Hi, Mama," he said sleepily. Sweat pasted the boy's blonde hair to his forehead, and indentations from his pillow tracked his flushed cheeks.

"Good morning, sweetheart." She planted a kiss on the top of his head and examined his face in an attempt to read his mood. He seemed to be in an obedient mind-set, so she said, "Go and fetch some milk from the keep, please. We'll have that with the bacon."

Instead of minding her, he sank onto a stool at the kitchen table. "I'm hungry, Ma. I'll fetch it after I eat some bacon."

Susannah frowned. "Caleb, I'm your mother. You must do what I say." She knew the words were hollow. Like her father before her, she never enforced her orders. One thing she couldn't bear was her son being unhappy, even for a moment, so she did everything in her power to indulge him, including letting him out of chores.

"I will fetch it, Ma, don't worry. But I'm gonna eat first," Caleb declared.

Susannah felt pressure building behind her eyes and burning in her nose. She tried to hold the tears back, but the frightening upcoming events of the day, combined with her out-of-control situation at home, caused her to lose her composure. The cabin was falling apart, the chickens weren't laying eggs, and her vegetable garden produced more weeds than carrots. She was about to marry a stranger, a frightening prospect on its own, but especially worrisome because of Caleb. She couldn't bear the thought of her future husband not liking her defiant boy, and Caleb didn't make it easy for strangers to like him.

As much as she loved her son, he was living proof of her sin and recklessness. A man whose greatest asset was his appearance had gotten her in the family way and then up and disappeared. He'd charmed her, and she'd seen none of his faults. Being irresponsible herself, she hadn't recognized that he too was irresponsible. The fact that he didn't ask her pa for permission to court her hadn't warned her of his character, since she'd never asked permission for anything either.

Her pregnancy had angered her father. He'd all but ignored Caleb, forcing Susannah to navigate the path of parenthood with little help. It was overwhelming for a woman like her, who in many ways was just a child herself. Her pregnancy also led her pa to change his will. The will still read that she would inherit the ranch, but a stipulation was inserted that she must be married within a year of his death or it would be forfeited to the bank. His death forced Susannah into a harsh reality. Not only did it necessitate her finding a husband, it also left her with a hole the size of Texas in her heart. Ben Smith had taken his last breath still disappointed in the daughter he'd doted on all her growing-up years.

His intentions in modifying the will were not wholly punitive. He hadn't wanted his daughter to be alone with a child and, because she was a fallen woman, he thought a man would only marry her if in doing so he would own a ranch. That reason for forcing her hand made Susannah feel even more ashamed.

"I'm sorry, Ma!" Caleb said, jumping to his feet. He rushed to her and wrapped his chubby arms around her waist. "I'll get the milk now. Don't cry, Mama. Please?"

Susannah's heart filled with love. Her son was a handful, but he was also darn sweet. She would do whatever it took to give him every happiness in life, beginning with making sure she married in time to prevent them from losing everything.

* * *

Susannah hopped down from the buggy, sending a small cloud of dust into the air. She quickly shook it out of her pink calico skirt. She adjusted her hat, which sprouted a feather plume, and lifted her chin, trying to trick herself into feeling confident about what was about to take place.

Caleb was back at home with the foreman's daughter Betsy so that Susannah could engage in the activities of the day freely. Despite this short, rare bit of freedom, she felt trapped. Her fate was sealed with whatever waited for her on the other side of the hotel's dining room door.

She spotted her friend Mary standing outside the hotel wringing her hands. Mary was one of the few women in town who didn't look down her nose at Susannah. When Susannah approached her, she took hold of her hands and gave them a squeeze. "I'll pray for you."

Her friend's words provided Susannah with the opposite of comfort. "How did it go, getting all the men settled into the dining room?"

17

Mary shifted her gaze away and shrugged. "They were surprised to find out about each other, I suppose."

It seemed to Susannah there was something Mary wasn't saying. She thought about trying to pry the information out of her, but decided against it. She was already beginning to lose her nerve and didn't think it a good idea to stall for answers.

After thanking her friend, Susannah gathered the fabric of her skirts in one hand and strode with purpose to the hotel's dining room door, where she waited outside for a moment to gather her courage.

She heard a loud male voice through the thin door. "Where the hell is this shickster? I want to see if she looks as racked in real life as she does in that photograph."

Susannah stiffened with alarm. No one could accuse her of being a prude, but hearing a man speak so flippantly about her body, which was perfectly covered in the photograph she had provided the men, gave her a sinking feeling in her gut. What if these men were exactly like the men in town who had treated her like a fallen woman who didn't deserve respect?

Perhaps the man who had spoken was the only one with ill manners, she told herself. She hadn't heard the other men laugh or say anything in response. With that realization providing a sliver of hope, she squared her shoulders, opened the door, and walked inside.

Silence met her upon her entrance. Four sets of eyes stared at her as she examined each of the men openly. They were all cowboys like they had communicated in their letters. They appeared typically rough and strong, but they had taken care to look somewhat presentable. Three were clean-shaven, and the fourth had a short beard that was neatly trimmed. All removed their hats from their heads upon her entrance.

Her throat felt dry and she swallowed hard. When she spoke, it was with far less confidence than she would have preferred. She croaked, "I would like to know which of you spoke crudely of my appearance. I overheard what you said from outside the door."

Only one of the men dropped his gaze, so she knew the answer without him admitting it. "Was it you?" she asked. He looked about her age or even a little younger.

He circled his Stetson in his hands. "Yes, that was me. I suppose you won't be fixin' to pick me then," he said sullenly, sounding resigned to his imminent rejection.

"You suppose right," she responded primly. She moved aside so that he could exit the room.

He left looking like a whipped dog, and Susannah felt a burst of courage. She was in control of this situation, she reminded herself, and there were still three men to choose from. She returned her attention to the men left standing.

"As you can see, I responded to several of you saying I would accept your proposal and marry you in order that you might run the ranch left to me by my late father, but obviously, I will only choose one of you today and the rest of you will need to return to where you came from."

One of the three cowboys smiled and stepped forward. "I'd like to introduce myself. I'm Ezra Manning. If you recall from my letter, I said I grew up on a ranch."

He was thin, and his smile held insecurity. She liked that he was not overly confident, for that meant he would likely do her bidding at the ranch, if she chose him.

Susannah returned the smile and held out her hand. "I'm delighted to meet you, Mr. Manning, and all the rest of you as well."

Ezra brought her knuckles to his lips and kissed them. She squashed the urge to wipe her hand on her frock. "We're delighted to meet you too, Miss Smith."

"Speak for yourself," a deep voice interjected. "I, for one, am less than delighted to meet a woman who thinks nothing of deceiving four men."

Susannah looked up with surprise at the man who had spoken. He had placed his Stetson back on his head and was glaring at her with his hands on his hips. She opened her mouth to speak, but no words came out. The tetchy man was very handsome. One of his brows quirked up over his dark eyes as he regarded her, giving him a sardonic appearance that hinted at how absurd he found his current predicament. His clothes were plain, but clean. A white, long-sleeved shirt hugged broad shoulders and strong arms under a suede vest. His trousers were typical for a cowboy, rough brown wool that was faded at his knees as a result of use.

"This is some trick, young lady, making us all think we were comin' here to get hitched and take possession of a ranch, when instead you wish us to compete to win your favor." He shook his head and walked past her toward the door. "I don't want any part of this blasted circus."

"Wait!" Susannah cried. "I'm sorry, truly, but I was afraid people might lie in their letters. I felt it necessary to take this precaution."

He looked at her over his shoulder and scoffed. "I can see why you were afraid. People who are dishonest expect others to behave the same."

She flinched. His remark stung, both because it made her feel guilty and because of the three men left in the room, he was the one she was most attracted to. A voice inside her head told her to let him go. A man like this would never be indulgent toward her, and he didn't seem likely to do her bidding either. Still, she wanted to be the one to choose against him, not the other way around, so she desperately fought to keep him there for the time being.

"I'm not dishonest normally, I promise," she said. "I'm all alone in the world and feel I must make wise decisions. Please stay, sir, and do try to forgive me. At least hear what I have to say."

She watched his broad back expand as he drew a deep breath. She held her own breath until finally, he turned and walked to a chair, sat down, and took off his Stetson, which he placed on his bent knee. "Very well, Miss Smith. It's not like I have anywhere else to be."

Susannah had determined while preparing for this day that it was an easygoing demeanor and ranching experience that were most important to her in a man. She was not supposed to care about a man's looks, as that had gotten her into a world of trouble with her last beau, and she most certainly was not to choose a man who was as strict as this one appeared to be about good behavior.

While she was gaping at the man who was wrong for her, noticing how his thick mop of brown hair was combed neatly to match his trimmed beard, the other man in the room introduced himself. "I'm Clayton," he said, holding out his hand.

Distracted, Susannah shook it. A glance at him showed that he was very uncomfortable with the current situation, but he didn't seem displeased with her like Mr. Wrong, which she now knew using the process of elimination to be Adam Harrington.

"Nice to meet you, Clayton," she said, hardly looking at him. An awkward silence followed. She felt her cheeks growing warm as she struggled to think of something to say. All of the questions she'd prepared now seemed unnecessary, since she no longer felt like she was giving an interview to select a candidate. Rather, she felt like she must prove her own worth.

"Please sit down, gentlemen," she said to Clayton and Ezra. Adam was already sitting. Either he was unaware that a man should stand in a lady's presence when she was standing, or he didn't consider her a lady. Whichever it was, it was disconcerting to Susannah, and she felt her stomach tighten into nervous knots as she took her seat across from the men.

Adam hadn't removed his hard gaze from her face. He wasn't glowering at her, exactly—more like studying—but the intensity she felt radiating from him made it difficult for her to concentrate.

She cleared her throat. "I haven't yet thanked you for making the journey to meet me, so let me begin with that. Please know that you all have my heartfelt thanks."

Adam let out something that sounded like a snort of amusement. Clayton and Ezra nodded at her in what appeared to be a forgiving manner. *Choose Clayton or Ezra*, Susannah told herself firmly. *These are men who will go easy on you, who will do your bidding.*

She drew a deep breath and continued. "What you know about me is true. I am in possession of chattel and land that require the attention of a rancher. I cannot simply hire someone to tend to the ranch. The reason he must be my husband is because it was stipulated by my father in his will that in order to keep the ranch, I must be married. Still, it is my ranch and you will be working for me."

She reached into her satchel and pulled out the deed, which included a map with the ranch's dimensions, and handed it to Ezra, requesting that he pass it around when he finished. Each man studied the deed carefully, ending with Adam, who studied it the longest and then handed it back to her.

"Please tell me a little about yourselves, gentlemen," Susannah said in as cheerful a voice as she could muster, hoping to remove some of the focus from herself.

Clayton and Ezra took turns sharing their experiences, while Adam remained quiet. Susannah barely heard either of them because she was squirming under Adam's gaze. She became sharply aware of her own body as her breasts rose and fell with each shallow breath. When she noticed suddenly that the room was silent, she addressed Adam. "What about you, Mr. Harrington? What is your experience?"

He rubbed the back of his neck. His voice was friendlier than she would have guessed it would be when he spoke. "I've been involved in ranching since I was a lad, Miss Smith. I inherited a plot of land from my father and worked it hard for nearly a decade. Unfortunately, sheepherders took over Amarillo. I got to scrapping with several of them over my father's land, and since it wasn't written anywhere that the land was mine, the sheepherders won, slowly crowding the cattle away from the most fertile parts. In general the cattlemen in Amarillo got swindled. I wasn't the only one. We were outnumbered and without the protection of the law, which meant I needed to either become a sheepherder myself or start over in a new place. That's the long and short of it." He stretched out his legs, leaned back in his chair, and crossed his boots at the ankle.

Though he hadn't said anything remarkable, it was the most he had spoken, and Susannah found herself drawn to the sound of his voice. It was a calm, deep drawl, and she sensed that there wasn't a dishonest bone in his body. He spoke with forthrightness and humility, and though he had every reason to be bitter about losing his father's ranch on account of sheepherders, he didn't sound like he carried a chip on his shoulder.

His legs looked powerful, she noticed, and then blushed at the strange thought. Though no stranger to lust, she'd never felt such a strong and immediate attraction toward someone, such that even the sight of him stretching his legs caused her stomach to flutter. She wondered what it would be like to sit on a lap like that and to have the big man's arms wrap around her and hold her close. She guessed she would feel safe. She hadn't felt safe since her father's death, and a man's protection wasn't something she'd considered looking for. Now that she felt like it might be within her reach, it was mighty appealing.

This man will take over everything. He will not do your bidding. He's not what you want, the voice inside her head harped. But, like she'd done many times before in her life, she ignored her voice of reason.

"I would like to make my decision," she said softly, looking at Adam. "Before I do, though, I'm wondering if anyone in the room would not care to accept me, should I choose him."

She glanced at Clayton and Ezra. As she had predicted, both agreed that they would be honored if she chose them. She then looked at Adam and held her breath. Never had she felt more vulnerable than she did at that moment, waiting for his verdict.

Adam uncrossed his legs and sat up into a less-relaxed pose. He dropped his gaze to the floor with a frown and appeared to be deep in thought. Susannah could hardly handle the suspense. She wrung her hands and then fiddled with the lace stitched onto her sleeves as she waited.

Finally, he lifted his head and spoke gently after catching her eye. "If you choose me, Miss Smith, I will accept. But after that, you and I will have a very serious discussion about honesty, and that discussion will not be pleasant for you."

Chapter Three

A shiver went through Susannah, equal parts delight and anticipation. Adam seemed very serious about scolding her for her deception, and though the thought of it certainly was unsavory, she felt pleased that he had indicated he would accept her. She smiled a victorious smile. "I wish to choose you, Mr. Harrington." She studied him for a sign of happiness over her decision, but he didn't show any.

"You may not wish it after our discussion, Miss Smith," he said ominously, his eyes piercing hers.

Susannah felt a moment of doubt. Was she making a horrible, irreversible mistake? Maybe she should have listened to that voice in her head.

Before she could ponder that further, Adam said, "Apologize and say goodbye to the other gentlemen." His voice had taken an authoritative edge.

Another tremor went through her. A voice of authority was not something she wanted. No, no, no. She wanted to be in charge. She would have to get her control back somehow, but first things first. Holding out her hand to the two rejected men, she bade them farewell and told them she was sorry for lying. She really did feel guilty, though perhaps not as guilty as Adam thought she should feel.

When the men had left and she and Adam were alone in the room, he said in a low, firm voice, "Lock the door, Susannah."

Hearing her Christian name roll off his tongue made her heart flutter in her chest, and she felt the stirrings of romantic excitement. If he wanted privacy, what was he planning? Perhaps he would take her into his arms and kiss her. Her stomach tightened and a tremor of nervous desire swept over her. She locked the door as instructed and turned to face him.

This was not happening at all how she had imagined. What she'd pictured in her mind was a long day of giving instructions to the man she chose, ending in a wedding ceremony. Now, though, one glance at Adam's face told her she was not the one in control, and nothing was certain anymore.

It wasn't long before he instructed her again. "Come here and lie over my lap for our discussion, Susannah."

She quirked her head to the side, confused. It was a strange way to ask her to sit on his lap. The prospect of it delighted her though. She'd already imagined being wrapped up in his arms while supported by his strong legs. She walked toward him without hesitation, noticing the censure in his gaze deepen as she grew nearer. But she did not allow his stern expression to discourage her.

She felt hopeful that he would soon forgive her deception. After all, she had chosen him and she was beautiful. He didn't yet know about her reputation or her son, so he couldn't judge her for those things yet. One step at a time.

When she reached where he was sitting, she sat down on his lap quite provocatively and draped her arms around his neck, causing her bosom to be positioned centimeters from his face. He was to be her husband, and she had no desire to be coy with him. She drew a deep breath that raised her breasts to touch his chin and stared dolefully into his eyes, sincerely believing that her feminine wiles would cause the discussion to be less severe, if not forgotten altogether.

He inhaled sharply and closed his eyes for a moment, showing her that he was not unaffected by the close proximity of her body, but when he opened them, they were gleaming with disapproval. She saw lust there, too, but his jaw was set in determination not to allow it to sway him from the "discussion."

"I said to lie *over* my lap, woman, not sit on it. You're a peck and a half of trouble, aren't you?" He pushed her off, took hold of her arm, and bent her over his knees face down. It happened so fast that it took a moment for her understanding to catch up with his actions. By the time she realized he intended to spank her, he'd tossed up her pretty pink skirt and petticoat. Susannah's legs flailed in the air and her palms touched the floor. For a moment she felt like she was going to fall, but his large left hand curled firmly around her side and held her in place.

"Mr. Harrington!" she cried, squirming. "Surely you don't intend to…" She couldn't even say the word. Her face felt hot as her blood drained down to it and she could hear her heartbeat pumping in her ears.

"…spank you?" he finished. "That's exactly what I intend to do, provided that you accept it. Do you agree to accept my discipline for your deception?" He placed his right hand on her bottom, covered only by frilly drawers, which caused her to squeal. A current of need shot through her body. She hadn't enjoyed a man's touch in quite some time, and feeling his strong hand atop an intimate place made her long to be touched more. She did *not* want to be spanked, however, and he didn't seem to have any other objective in mind.

She ran through her options and couldn't find a single way out of her predicament. She had already rejected the other men. But how could she agree to suffer something so humiliating from the man who would be her husband? Hot tears came to her eyes and she sniffled. Adam's hand came down in a hard swat that made her gasp in surprise and lift her head.

"I asked you a question," he said, his voice stern. "I expect an answer. Will you accept my discipline, yes or no?"

She shifted a little. Her husband-to-be was far, far stricter than she wanted. She should have listened to that voice in her head! She was used to being spoiled and treated delicately, not manhandled in such a way!

"What if I say no, Mr. Harrington?" she asked. She knew the answer, but she wanted to delay him and in doing so give her time to process the situation.

"If you say no, I will place you right side up and bid you farewell. I will also be disappointed, as I do very much want this to work between us. I won't have a dishonest, inconsiderate wife, though, and I need to know you can accept consequences."

Tears of frustration flooded her eyes. Her father had only spanked her once when she was a child, with his belt, and it had hurt terribly, but then he had forgiven her. Perhaps that would be the case with Adam as well. Maybe it wouldn't be too bad.

"I will accept," she whimpered tearfully. "Please don't hurt me too much."

"Are you already crying, Susannah?" he asked, sounding amazed.

"Yes," she said honestly. She squeezed her eyes shut in anticipation of the next smack.

Instead, he rubbed her bottom in circles, causing arousal to intermingle with her anxiety. "A spanking is supposed to hurt, but the pain doesn't last. Surely it's not worth so many tears."

"I'm scared and embarrassed," she whimpered.

"Yeah?" he asked lightly and without sounding the least bit sympathetic. He brought his hand down in another smack, harder this time, causing her to emit a surprised squeak.

"How do you think I felt when I realized I'd dropped everything to become a candidate in a foolish woman's game of chance? And how do you suppose those other men feel right now?" He spanked her hard twice more and then waited for a response.

His words hurt worse than his hand, which hurt plenty too. She hadn't considered that the men were out anything but time. "I'm sorry," she said mournfully. "Honest, I am."

He resumed spanking her, this time not letting up after a few swats. Every smack was punishing and delivered on the fleshiest part of her cheeks. "As you should be, Miss Smith. I'd like you to answer the question. How do you suppose those men feel?"

"I don't know!" she cried. Her husband-to-be spanked *hard*. Every stroke of his hand caused her to jerk forward, tangling her carefully brushed hair around her face.

"You do know. You just said how you feel. Repeat that to me, for you are not the only one to feel it."

"S-scared and embarrassed?" she stammered, shifting over his lap.

"That's right, Miss Smith. Now, I can't say as I blame you for wanting a few men to choose from, but you should have said that in your letters. You should've been honest with us."

She sniffled. "I know."

"And I imagine those men have lost a lot more than the ability to sit for a few minutes, which is your only punishment. Quite lenient in comparison, wouldn't you say?"

It was horrible, hearing him scold her. She felt like he didn't like her at all and was disappointed in his decision to stay. "Please!" she wailed. "Will you be able to forgive me? I don't want you to hate me if you're going to be my husband."

He paused, resting his punishing hand on her clenching cheeks. He then chuckled, which surprised her, since he was acting so strict with her.

Her face grew even warmer, and a bolt of anger shot through her. "You think I'm a joke. You think this is hilarious, me being in pain and humiliated."

"No, I certainly don't," he argued, and resumed spanking her firmly, causing her to squeal and squirm in his iron grip.

"Ow ow *OWW*," she protested.

"I don't think this is funny, and I don't think you're a joke. I think you're naughty. And I think you need to be taught a lesson."

"I've learned it!" she informed him, as his hand continued to descend on her poor seat.

"You worrying about me hating you tells me you haven't often received correction. That's why I laughed. Am I right about that? Is it rare for you to be spanked?"

Mercifully, he paused to listen to her. She looked back at him over her shoulder. His brow quirked up at her as he leveled her with his gaze. He looked so very handsome and serious that she temporarily forgot to be outraged over the punishment. She gave him a small nod and whispered, "Yes, it's rare. I've only been spanked once before."

He nodded in understanding and resumed the spanking. She groaned and looked back down at the ground, her hair spilling around her face.

"Your undisciplined days have come to an end, Miss Smith. I won't have a spoiled, misbehaving wife, so you will suffer correction if you're mine. I am assuming, of course, that you still want to marry me after this punishment is finished. I could be wrong to make that assumption."

"I'll still marry you, Mr. Harrington, and I will accept your correction," she said in a resigned voice. What choice did she have, really?

"I'm glad to hear that, but you might want to wait until I'm finished spanking you to answer. I'm going to remove your drawers now to apply the rest of the correction to your bare bottom."

Alarm gripped her. "No!" she shrieked, wriggling and frantically trying to get up. "I can't bear that, Mr. Harrington!"

To her surprise and relief, he released his hold on her and allowed her to stand. Her skirts were still bunched up around her waist, and her hands flew to clutch her smarting bottom. She faced Adam but couldn't meet his eyes. Taking in a shuddering breath, she tried to blink back tears. The tears were mostly from embarrassment, if she was honest with herself. The spanking wasn't without pain, but her bottom didn't hurt too terribly now that he'd stopped spanking it.

"Compose yourself, Miss Smith," Adam said sternly.

She gathered her courage and peered at him through wet, lowered lashes. Though his voice had been firm, she could see compassion in his eyes and felt a little better. She had been afraid he would find her ridiculous and view her with contempt, but there was no mockery in his gaze—only mild sternness.

All feelings of relief quickly vanished when he spoke again. "You know you've earned this. Now come back over my knee. If you hadn't made such a fuss, it would be nearly over by now."

"Please, Mr. Harrington," she pled. "Please don't take down my drawers." She rushed to think of an excuse and quickly found one. Proper women didn't disrobe for a man before marriage. She wasn't proper, of course, but he didn't know that yet. She lifted her chin and said with more confidence than she felt, "It isn't right since we aren't yet married. I promise I have learned my lesson."

He narrowed his eyes at her. She did her best to look contrite, and she was certain the tears aided her in doing so. Most men's hearts softened when a woman cried, and she could only hope that Mr. Harrington's did too.

"Oh, all right," he relented. "I'll give you a choice. You may either do as you're told and come back over my knee where I will apply a few swats to your misbehaving bare ass, or I can finish this after we are married so that it will be deemed proper. Up to you."

"After we're married," she said immediately. She believed that she would be able to convince him not to finish the spanking that night. If he was anything like other men, he would prefer to engage in other activities—much more pleasurable activities—with her naked body.

"Very well," he said, giving her a short nod.

She arranged her skirts to cover her bottom and wiped her wet cheeks with the backs of her hands. When she lifted teary eyes to meet his, she noticed that his gaze was kind.

"You all right?"

"Yes, sir."

34

A slow smile appeared on his handsome face, displaying a dimple that looked quite boyish compared to the rest of him, which looked hard and manly. "My, my, a walloping really straightens you out, doesn't it? That spanking wasn't even very hard, and yet suddenly you're as sweet as a little kitten."

"I beg to differ," she said with a pout.

His grin widened. "About what, kitten? That you're sweet or that you're straightened out?" His voice had a tease in it.

"You know what I mean! It was a very hard spanking," she exclaimed in a fit of temper, feeling like he was making fun of her and not liking it one bit.

"Oh, it was not. Barely a pat and a tickle." He rose and held out his bent elbow to her. "How about if we go get something to eat and get to know each other a bit? As much as I want to keep staring at your pretty face and tendin' to your fragile feelings, I'm hungry and in need of some chow."

Susannah's hurt pride faded away. She reached out tentatively and hooked her hand in his elbow. She looked up at him, craning her neck. He was practically a giant. She liked that.

"You think I have a pretty face, Mr. Harrington?" She was shamelessly fishing for compliments, but she thought she deserved a little sweet-talking after what she had just endured.

Much to her pleasure, he indulged her. "I'm not blind. You have a pretty *everything*, darlin'." He smiled and clapped his Stetson on his head. "Perhaps it's best I didn't lower your drawers. Your sweet little bare bottom may have been my undoing."

Susannah flushed with happiness at the strange compliment. Maybe this wasn't a bad choice, after all. He might be strict, but boy was he charming. "You're very handsome yourself, Mr. Harrington," she said, allowing him to lead her out of the hotel's dining room.

As he led her, she shook her head. He wasn't supposed to be leading. *She* was. Sakes alive, what had she gotten herself into?

Chapter Four

The rest of the day was spent happily, culminating in a short ceremony that bound them together as man and wife. The more Susannah spoke to Adam, the more she liked him. He behaved gallantly, pulling out her chair for her and standing when she stood. They talked easily like they were old friends, and she delighted in the merriment she saw in his eyes. She could tell that he found her very beautiful, which was not at all surprising since most men did, but he also seemed to genuinely like her.

When Adam looked into her eyes and vowed to stay by her side in sickness and in health, Susannah's heart filled with hope. However, in the back of her mind throughout the day and while they exchanged vows was the knowledge that Adam did not yet know her reputation in town for being a fallen woman. She knew he would discover it eventually, and she could only pray it was after he became totally smitten with her. She used every trick of seduction she knew, brushing up against him lightly, smiling coyly, stroking his ego and hanging on his every word.

On the way to the cabin after the ceremony, he drove the buggy, another gesture of leadership she hadn't anticipated. During the first part of the journey, she kept up the lighthearted conversation they had enjoyed most of the day, but as they grew closer to the home they would share together with her son, the realization that Adam was going to find out about Caleb filled her with fear. She searched for the right words to say to him, to prepare him for something she should have mentioned much sooner. Would he dislike raising a son who wasn't his? When they lay together that night, would he be disappointed to discover she wasn't a virgin? It was dizzying to think about all that could go wrong.

It turned out that her new husband was attentive and noticed the change in her demeanor. "You're awfully quiet," he said, glancing over at her. "It's been a long day. Are you tired?"

It was dark, and she could only see the outline of his profile, but his voice was kind and she could imagine that he was looking at her kindly too. It made her feel wretched. He was about to find out that she had once again kept pertinent information from him. No doubt he would see this in an even worse light than her less-than-upstanding method for finding a husband.

"There's something I need to tell you," she lamented. She shifted in her seat and looked ahead, noticing that the cabin was fast approaching. She could already see the coal oil lamp that burned in the window.

"Tell me what's on your mind when we get settled," he suggested, slapping the reins on the horse to move her along at a faster clip.

"All right," she agreed, feeling a measure of relief at the excuse to delay the conversation for a bit longer. "The barn is just past the cabin if you want to drive the horse straight there."

The barn was dark, so Susannah lit a lamp when they arrived and showed Adam the tack bucket where the hoof picks and brushes were thrown together. She wondered if he would comment on the lack of organization, but he merely nodded and got to work.

She picked up one of the worn brushes, but he stopped her. "You go sit on the bench. I'll take care of the horse."

She bristled. He was in her barn, already giving her instructions, and even though the instructions were favorable, they felt strange. Once again, she had been expecting to instruct him and the opposite had taken place.

"I can help," she offered. "The foreman does most of the work with the horses, but I'm not useless around them."

He shook his head, and his tone brooked no argument when he responded. "You can help by pouring me some whiskey when we get inside. This here is men's work."

She slowly placed the brush back in the bucket. "As you wish," she said with a shrug. Susannah sat on the bench and folded her hands in her lap. She could have argued with him. She could have informed him that she was perfectly capable of helping him with the horse—it was her horse, after all—but the truth of the matter was that in that moment, she felt happy to give up control and have someone else see to things. During the last year, she had felt every responsibility weighing heavily on her shoulders.

She watched Adam unbuckle the straps of the harness from the mare. He moved expertly around the horse and within ten minutes she was brushed, her hooves were picked, and she was relegated to a stall with fresh hay, water, and a bag of oats.

"I can see you know about horses," she complimented.

"Yes, ma'am, I wasn't just shootin' my mouth off when I said I grew up on a ranch."

"Seems I made a good choice when I picked you."

He laughed. "Funny, I was just thinking the same thing, Mrs. Harrington. Well, I mean I was thinking I made a good choice accepting."

She smiled, liking the sound of her new name coming from the lips of her new husband. "I hope you continue to think you made a good choice."

"I will. Nobody is perfect. But the fact is, you have just made me the luckiest man on God's green earth. A wife and a ranch—it's just about all I ever wanted."

She warmed to his words and wished she could bask in them, but there was still one important issue he was unaware of. Until he accepted the fact that she had a son outside of wedlock, she could not be at ease. "Is there anything else you want, Adam? Children, perhaps?"

He didn't answer right away, which made Susannah nervous, and when he spoke his words filled her with fear. "No, I've never really wanted children. Do you?"

Oh, God. He doesn't even want his own *children?* "Yeah, maybe just one," she answered with wry despair.

"We can talk about that. I might be persuaded to change my mind. Now come along, darlin'," he said, holding out his hand to her. "I'll have that whiskey now and you can tell me what's goin' on in that head of yours. Then we have the rest of your spanking to attend to."

She let out a small squeak of alarm. She'd forgotten about his promise to finish the spanking on her bare backside. She had convinced herself hours ago that he too would forget, but it seemed that was not the case. Strangely, the prospect of receiving Adam's discipline appealed to her in that moment. If he spanked her after she told him about her son, she would almost be grateful. That would mean there was a chance he'd forgive her.

She rose, placed her hand in his, and allowed him to lead her to the cabin. He carried in his other hand his lone piece of luggage and set it next to the front door upon entering. The house was quiet, which meant Caleb was asleep in the back room. Betsy, the foreman's daughter tasked with watching her son that day, was snoozing on the sofa and awoke when they entered the room. She gawked at Adam unabashedly before Susannah ushered her outside.

They spoke on the porch. "He's awful handsome, ma'am," Betsy exclaimed in a high-pitched, girlish voice.

Susannah felt proud upon hearing the girl's compliment. Her husband was indeed handsome, and he was hers... at least for now. He might very well hightail it back to Texas after her big secret came to light.

"Does he have good table manners? That's important, you know. You don't want a man who eats with his knife."

Susannah laughed in spite of her nerves. "There are much more important qualities to seek in a husband besides his looks and table manners. But yes, his manners are quite all right."

Betsy shook her head stubbornly. "I couldn't marry a man who ate with his knife. No, ma'am."

"That's fine, Betsy. That's fine. I'm sure you will find a gentleman when you start courtin'." Susannah shooed the girl along home so she could get the next part of the evening over with. She watched as Betsy trotted to her parents' cabin that was just within view. With a sigh of relief at having her gone, Susannah gathered her courage for what lay ahead and walked inside.

She came to a dead stop as soon as she entered, and her mouth fell open. Adam was sitting on the sofa with a bewildered expression focused on Caleb, who had plopped down next to him and was chattering about his day.

"I stacked the blocks this high," Caleb said excitedly, holding his hand in the air to demonstrate.

Adam raised an eyebrow. "Is that right?"

Caleb nodded and then noticed she was in the room. "Hi, Mama!" he exclaimed. "Is this my new pa?"

Adam's eyes widened with shock and the blood drained out of his face. It would have been funny if it weren't so tragic. Susannah swallowed hard. She didn't know what to say and felt her nose burning. She was close to tears and feared that speaking would release them. She knew she had to say something, but she struggled to sort through her emotions. She found it touching to see Caleb with Adam. It was close to the most beautiful thing in the world to behold. Intermixed with those soft feelings was one of sheer terror. How would she ever explain this?

Before she could find any words, Adam cleared his throat and answered Caleb. "Yes, I reckon I am your new pa, kid, and you and me have lots to talk about. But your mama and I need to talk right now, so get yourself back to bed. You can tell me more about your toys when the sun comes up."

Adam didn't know how difficult the child was, or else he may have been more forceful in his command. Rather, he instructed him as a man would to a child he was certain would obey him.

Susannah held her breath and willed Caleb to do as he was told the first time, for once. *Please, please be good*, she said to him silently.

"I can stay up a little longer," he informed Adam cheerfully. "I'm not sleepy at all."

Susannah groaned to herself, and Adam glanced at her with a questioning look.

"Caleb," she said, trying to hold her voice steady. "It's past your bedtime. Go to your room and I'll be there shortly to tuck you in."

Caleb's smile faded. His hands balled up into fists and his face reddened, indicating he was moments away from bursting into angry tears. *Not now, not tonight*, she despaired.

43

"It's not fair, Mama! I want to stay up and talk to my new pa. Why do you get to talk to him and I don't?"

She didn't know how to proceed. Normally she would wait for him to be through with his tantrum and then try to reason with him, but now that her parenting skills, or lack thereof, were being scrutinized by her new husband, she felt unsure.

It was Adam who took control of the situation. He stood and held out his hand to the angry little boy. "It's time for bed, Caleb," he said in a firm voice that made the boy's angry expression disappear as quickly as it had arrived. He stared up at the big man before slowly placing his chubby little hand into Adam's large one.

Caleb continued to gape until Adam said in mock impatience, "You'll have to lead me to your room, kid. I don't know where it is. Chop-chop."

Caleb let out a delighted giggle and then tugged Adam toward the back of the cabin. Susannah followed along behind them, a silent witness to the whole exchange.

"This is my bed," Caleb told Adam proudly.

"It's a very nice bed," Adam said, apparently hearing the pride in the child's voice. He unfolded the quilt and motioned for Caleb to get in. Much to Susannah's surprise, Caleb obeyed right away. Adam tucked the covers around him and tousled his hair. "Goodnight, kid." He moved aside and glared at Susannah. If looks could kill, the look he leveled at her would have struck her dead right then and there.

She managed to go through the motions of saying goodnight to her child by habit. She bent and kissed his forehead, then followed Adam, who had already stalked out of the room and was waiting for her just outside of the door.

Chapter Five

Adam closed the bedroom door softly behind her and walked to the sitting room, where he paced and jerked a hand through his hair. "What in the blazes, woman?" His voice was low but filled with heat.

Susannah burst into the tears she'd successfully held back until that moment. "I know I should have told you."

"You don't say?" he hissed. "Where's his father?" He approached her and stood in front of her with his hands on his hips. His glower felt like a slap in the face.

"I don't know!" she moaned. "He up and left before Caleb was even born. I haven't seen him since."

"You didn't get a divorce? You're still married?" Adam exclaimed, his voice becoming louder.

"No!" She felt herself swaying on her feet, like she might very well pass out. "His father and I were never married."

A long silence followed, during which Susannah felt utter despair. She covered her face with her hands, unable to bear looking at him.

She started when he took hold of her wrists and pried her hands away from her face. The touch was gentle despite him being obviously angry. She kept her eyes downcast.

"You should have told me," he growled. "Anything else I should know about? Do you have a body buried in the cellar? Have you robbed a bank or stolen a horse?"

She worked up the courage to look at him. Staring pleadingly into his flashing eyes, she said, "No, this is the last big secret. I promise. You wouldn't have married me if I told you. I couldn't take the chance that you would change your mind if you knew I was a fallen woman."

"I still would have married you," he snarled, dropping her wrists.

She didn't believe him. "I doubt that very much!" she said, feeling a rush of anger. "After you spanked me for being dishonest, here you are lying to me."

"I guess you'll never know, will you?" he said tersely. "You didn't give me the chance to prove what kind of man I am. I'm not the kind to go back on my word. You really are something else." He shook his head and stormed to the sofa, where he sat down. Silence filled the room until he bellowed, "Now would be a good time for that whiskey!"

Relieved to have an opportunity to please him in a small way, Susannah rushed to the kitchen's keep, where she pulled out the half-full bottle. She could use some bottled courage herself. For a fleeting moment, she wondered if she shouldn't drink in front of Adam. After all, it was unladylike and vulgar for a woman to drink a man's brew, but she shrugged and poured herself a glass. Might as well, since he already thought lowly of her.

She returned to the sitting room and handed Adam his glass, her hand brushing up against his as she did and sending tingles throughout her body. He raised an eyebrow at the glass of whiskey she'd poured for herself. "You're full of surprises, aren't you, Mrs. Harrington?" His voice was no longer angry, which filled her with relief. If anything, his tone was lighthearted.

She sat next to him gingerly and was glad when he accepted the nearness of her body without recoiling. "Are you still glad you married me, even after knowing this, Adam?"

Adam swallowed his sip of whiskey. "Yes, Susannah."

It was just two simple words, but they were spoken honestly and they meant more to her than he would ever know. Good feelings warmed her insides along with the whiskey. She felt the muscles in her face relaxing and easing into a smile. "Thank you."

"You deserve the spanking of your life for not telling me about your son," he declared, tossing the rest of the whiskey back. He set the glass on the table next to the sofa with a clink. "If ever a woman deserved a walloping, it would be you right now, but I feel more inclined to explain something to you."

She took another sip of liquor and fastened her eyes on him. She felt her stomach somersaulting at the prospect of being bare-bottomed over her husband's lap and feeling his discipline once again. She wasn't sure if it was more anxiety or arousal that was causing her body's reaction, but the feeling was strong, whatever it was.

Scrubbing a hand around his face, he said, "I never understood it, why folks look down on a woman who gets in the family way without a husband. Folks never blame the man, and I reckon that's mighty unfair."

She swallowed, marveling over his compassionate logic. She hadn't heard that kind of acceptance from anyone, and instead had been going through her days feeling defensive and constantly judged.

"I thought Caleb's father loved me, but he left me all alone. The townsfolk have had little to do with me because of my indiscretion. The women don't like me being around their husbands, and the men don't want to draw their wives' ire."

Adam shook his head. "So you've been alone. Has anyone watched out for you and Caleb since your father died?"

"The foreman, Timothy. He keeps the ranch going."

"Well, that's something. I reckon I'll be meeting Timothy tomorrow, when I'll be going to the range. I hope we get along."

"I think you will," Susannah assured him. "But…" She hesitated before continuing. "The plan was for him to stay in charge and for you to just kind of follow his directions and mine." She looked down at the empty whiskey glass in her hand.

Adam reached out and took her glass away slowly. "I'm not the kind of man you intended on picking, am

I?" He set her glass down next to his on the table and studied her, waiting for a response.

She shook her head and answered honestly. "No."

"You wanted someone weaker-willed, who would be swayed by your feminine charms and do your bidding. That's how you're used to getting your way with men."

Her mouth fell open and she stared at him, shocked at how bluntly he had put it. Of course, that was exactly the setup she'd envisioned, but she didn't think she'd made it quite that obvious. And it sure made her sound like an awful person.

His mouth quirked up to one side, revealing his dimple. "The look on your face answers my question. It's all right. You aren't the kind of woman I intended on marrying either, but here we are. We will make the best of it."

She felt a sinking in her gut. "Not the kind of woman… Because I'm not an innocent?" she inquired.

He nodded. "That, and I didn't plan to have a child. This isn't at all what I had in mind." He swept his hand in the air.

A rush of anger flowed through her. "Well, at least you have a ranch now," she snarled, her voice heavy with sarcasm. "Sorry you have to put up with me and my son along with it, but seems to me you were in need of a place to hang your hat, and—"

"Hey!" he said sharply, cutting her off. "Hold your tongue."

She bit her lip and stopped talking, but her anger remained.

"I like children, but I never wanted any because I watched my brother and sister die. Bein' responsible for the life of a little one… well, it scares me. That's all."

"Oh," she said, feeling instantly regretful.

"Yes, 'oh'," he mimicked in a slightly mocking tone. With a raised eyebrow, he added, "You'd best learn to control that temper of yours around me. Your pa should have curbed your impulsive behavior a long time ago. Life would be going better for you if he had."

His scolding made her feel very young and very naughty. She'd felt that way more than once while in his authoritative presence. It wasn't entirely unpleasant, but it was a new experience and she found herself wishing for more praise from him and less disapproval.

"I'm looking forward to getting to know Caleb better tomorrow," Adam said, his voice gone back to friendly. "I'm sure it will all work out just fine."

"I know he will love having a man around to talk to," Susannah said with a hopeful smile.

He smiled back at her, and she watched with a fluttering heart as his eyes slowly changed from light to smoldering. "First things first," he said, his voice deepening. "Tomorrow is still a fair bit in the future, and I have a naughty wife to attend to tonight."

Warmth bloomed over her body. She very much wanted Adam to take her into his arms and kiss her soundly, but she knew he was likely referring to her spanking.

He stood and collected her hand in his. "Bedroom," he said, his voice even lower and filled with lust. His gaze raked down her body, branding it with his eyes and making it clear she would be his in every way before the sun came up.

With one of her hands captured in his, she picked up the lamp on the hearth with her free hand and walked with him across the hardwood floor into her bedroom, which was on the opposite side of the cabin from Caleb's. Their hands unlocked. While she set the lamp on her dresser, Adam attempted to close the door. "It's broken," she said apologetically. "Just lift it a little and…"

Before she could finish her sentence, he'd jammed it shut. "I'll see to that tomorrow," he told her, which infused her with gratefulness. She wondered if he knew how much a simple statement like that made her feel cared for. She didn't even have to order him to fix it, like she'd been planning to do.

He slid out of his vest and shirt, and Susannah could see the shadows of the muscles on his chest and abdomen. She salivated, her body already responding to his presence in the room where they would consummate their status as man and wife.

Adam took the two strides to the bed, sat down, and struggled out of his boots as she unbuckled and removed her own, along with her stockings. He set his shoes aside neatly against the wall. Susannah took in the sight of him. He wore only his trousers, which hugged his long, hard legs. His hands rested on his knees in a relaxed pose.

"Take off your clothes, Mrs. Harrington," he commanded softly.

She blinked and moved trembling hands to her dress's bodice. She fumbled with her buttons.

"Nervous?" he asked, a slight tease in his voice.

She glanced at him and smiled bashfully, and he chuckled. His tease lightened the mood and made her feel a little more relaxed. She unbuttoned the rest of her dress smoothly, gaining courage as she did. Holding it in place for a moment, she caught his eye, then let it drop gracefully to the ground. His gaze darkened as he took in the sight of her body, now covered only by her thin chemise and drawers.

"Come here, darlin'," he said, holding out his hand to her.

Though she knew punishment was first on the menu, she didn't hesitate to move in his direction. She felt a magnetic pull toward him, and being near him felt natural. When his hand enclosed around hers once again, she felt a tremor of delight, and it only increased when his hands enveloped her waist and he positioned her to stand between his knees.

"You are lovely." His hands lowered to her hips, where he located the tied ribbon holding her drawers in place. "I am a man of my word, which is why I'm first going to lower these for the rest of your spanking," he said, sliding them down. "But it will be a short chastisement."

Her breathing became shallow, and her nipples felt sore and hard from rubbing against her silk chemise.

"Step out," he said, and she obeyed so that he could remove the drawers completely. His hands trailed up the backs of her legs, and a whimper escaped her lips when his palms reached the underside of her buttocks. His hands felt warm, and she longed for him to caress her everywhere. He caught the hem of her chemise and slowly lifted it over her head. He tossed it aside, and she stood in front of him fully naked.

He groaned when he took in the complete sight of her, and he leaned forward to kiss each peaked nipple. The chill in the air intermingled with her arousal caused her to shiver, which he noticed. His lips spread into a sly smile. "Don't worry, darlin', I'm going to warm you up." He patted his leg. "You know what to do."

She moaned, feeling frantic with desire and also a bit irritated that even her naked body couldn't dissuade him from his disciplinary intent. A more compliant woman would have held her tongue, but Susannah said, "I very much wish you would make love to me instead of spanking me, Adam. That's what usually happens on the wedding night, you know."

His eyes narrowed. "I hope you're not arguing. This spanking has already been agreed upon."

She wanted him to kiss her. She wanted him to be worshiping her body, not disciplining her, and all her nervous energy and excitement aggravated her frustration. "I'm not arguing, I am commenting," she said petulantly. "I know you would prefer to make love to me too."

She reached out suddenly and pressed her hand between his legs to feel for the telltale sign of a man's desire, but she was not prepared for what she would discover. She gasped when her hand felt him through his trousers. He was already fully hard for her.

Catching her wrist, he pulled it away, and his eyes flashed dangerously. "Big mistake, kitten. You will pay dearly for that."

"Please," she said breathlessly. "Now I know it without a doubt. You want me." She licked her lips and nibbled at her bottom one, noticing how his eyes roamed down to see her movement.

"Right now I want you over my knee." He tugged her wrist south.

"Oh, fine," she huffed. "Get it over with then." She gave him a withering look before she fell over his leg with exaggerated obedience, lifting her bare bottom high in the air.

He slapped her ass immediately, very hard, and she squealed in protest, expecting him to at least let her settle first. "What was that?" she hissed.

He spanked her again, harder. "I was going to make this spanking pleasurable for you, since as you mentioned, it's our wedding night." He gripped her about the waist and fastened her against him as his hand fell hard and fast. "But you've made it quite clear you need to learn some discipline first, so there's been a change in plans."

"Owww," she cried, kicking her legs and wriggling. The slaps of his hand on her bare skin stung like nothing she'd ever experienced before. Gone was his teasing demeanor. Now she felt only his displeasure, and she didn't like it one bit. The spanking at the hotel had stung, but the current discipline stung much worse due to the removal of her drawers. Every spank felt like a burned branding.

"Did you learn nothing from earlier when you tried to seduce me instead of being apologetic over your deception?"

"I said I was sorry about that, Adam!"

"Oh yes, you were very sorry once the spanking began, and you're about to be very sorry once again. I can't believe you pulled the same trick twice."

"What trick?" she demanded, twisting in his lap angrily. "I wasn't pulling any trick!" This was simply not fair. Any normal man would be caressing her now, not causing her such agony.

"You most certainly were. Draping over me, pressing your breasts against me, and just now grabbing my cock like it's something you can lead me around by. That's not how this is going to work, wife. Trying to manipulate me will only get you spanked."

As much as she hated to admit it, he was right. That was exactly what she had tried to do. Her anger evaporated and she sunk over his lap in defeat, no longer stiffening or trying to avoid the swats. She hadn't wanted a man who would take charge, but that was exactly what she had gotten. She would have to get used to it, though she really wished he would be less strict.

He must have noticed her body's submission because the punishment ended after two more firm swats. He ran his hand over her smarting cheeks and then caressed them, rubbing out the sting. Within moments the burn transformed into a softer warmth that spread to her belly and caused an ache between her legs she hadn't felt in quite some time. She crushed her thighs together, surprised by how much her center burned for her new husband's attention.

"Your ass is so fucking gorgeous," he said, and squeezed each cheek.

She squeaked with surprise over the crude words, which ignited her desire. She had never wanted anything as desperately as she wanted him in that moment. "Please…" she whimpered.

He ran his hand down her thighs and brushed the sensitive flesh behind her knees. His fingers pressed between her legs and made their way back up again, spreading her legs apart as they did. "That's it," he murmured, as the spreading of his fingers caused her to open for him. His hand was soon inches from the apex of her legs, and she opened wider, inviting his touch.

With a lightness that differed sharply from the punishment his hand had inflicted on her bottom, he touched her swollen sex, letting out a low growl that made her stomach clench. "You liked it when I disciplined you, didn't you, kitten?" He ran a finger up her drenched slit to her clit and circled the aching nub gently. "You needed to be taught a lesson, hmm?"

His voice was as smooth as cream, and she felt herself gush onto his hand. "No," she whimpered. It was far too embarrassing to admit how aroused and submissive the discipline made her feel.

"Liar," he said mildly, giving her pussy a light spank before he continued to fondle her. As he did so in languorous strokes, she pressed her sex against him, needing to feel pressure, needing him inside of her. He removed his hand from where it was buried between her legs and smacked her bottom. "Get up on the bed. Lie on your back and spread your legs for me, kitten."

The instructions were so straightforward and obvious in intent that she almost laughed. She managed to stifle her giggles though, thankfully. She didn't want to take a chance that he would change his mind and force her to suffer the rest of the evening in unmet lust.

Scrambling to obey, she positioned herself in the center of the bed and rested the back of her head on the pillow. She allowed her knees to fall apart and watched his eyes darken. "It pleases me, you obeying like that," he said. "And I want to reward you. Tell me what you want, darlin'." He shucked off his trousers, bringing to her view his thick, erect manhood.

She licked her lips and trembled with anticipation as he approached. His calloused hands pressed the backs of her thighs, guiding her knees to her chest and exposing her sex obscenely in a way that was both humiliating and exhilarating. Her breath caught as he draped each of her legs carefully over his shoulders, then leaned forward and kissed her lips, stretching and opening her even wider. The pressure of his mouth against hers increased and her lips parted when his tongue gently insisted on entrance. Every bit of her felt open to him, her body a quivering, hopeful invitation. Their tongues intermingled and passion grew in her belly.

When his kiss moved to her neck, she answered his question in a whisper. "I want you."

"Good girl," he said approvingly, and the small praise ignited her desire. In that moment, she wanted to be his good girl, to please and submit to him, and she loved everything about being in his strong arms.

His cock pressed against her and, though she was fairly pinned in place, she moved toward him ever-so-slightly, a silent entreaty. When he entered her, she spasmed and the walls of her channel clutched him. It felt beyond good, beyond right. She needed more.

He fed her need and continued to push himself forward, splitting her into two halves made whole by him.

When he began fucking her in earnest, every stroke inside of her felt like both a caress and a demand, both a gift and a plundering.

She clung to him as the waves of pleasure washed over her, digging her fingernails into his back and crying out her release. He continued to pound into her until he stiffened and she felt him release his hot cum inside her.

"Criminy." He collapsed next to her, breathing hard.

She snuggled up against him, using the dip between his arm and chest as a pillow. They didn't speak for some time, the only sounds in the room their deep breaths and the distant howl of the foreman's dog.

Finally, Adam said in a tender voice, "Good night, wife."

She smiled and pulled the quilt up over them. She listened as his breathing become steady with sleep. She too found sleep shortly after, but before she did, she felt a wave of happiness over her choice and everything that had transpired that day. For the first time since she could remember, she felt some peace. Susannah hoped her contentment would never change, but there was still much she didn't know about her new husband and his methods for maintaining authority.

Chapter Six

Susannah was still asleep when Adam woke up at dawn as he did every morning, regardless of time or location. Ranching had attuned his body and mind to the necessity for light; he wouldn't have been able to sleep in if he'd tried. A chill was in the air, but the bed felt warm. Susannah's body was tucked into his chest naturally, as though they had been sleeping together for years and not hours. The nearby sound of a rooster's crow and a horse's nicker caused a sense of well-being and calm to flow through him. He felt like he was home, despite being hundreds of miles away from the only place he'd called home his entire life.

Reluctantly, he rolled away from Susannah. He stood to his feet, yawned, and stretched out his arms before looking down at the sleeping woman in the bed. She hadn't stirred. Without bothering to remain quiet, Adam dressed himself, washed his face using the frigid water in the basin on the dresser, and pulled on his boots. Still his bride remained immobile and silent as a rock.

He sat on the bed and observed her for a moment. She lay on her side, curled into a little ball facing away from him. Her light hair was tangled and fell over her face. The quilt only halfway covered her, revealing most of her slender bare back. He reached out and trailed a finger across her forehead, settling her messy hair away from her face. She sighed but still didn't wake up.

He felt the beginning of a smile. She looked quite sweet while she slept, and he hesitated to wake her, but it was time to begin the day. He needed her to fix him some coffee and breakfast so that he could get to work. He'd never known a woman to wait until after dawn to awaken. The women he knew would see to the tasks of lighting a fire and getting breakfast ready for their husbands, and he had assumed Susannah would do the same.

He placed a hand on her shoulder and shook her gently. "Susannah? Time to get up."

She groaned without opening her eyes and pulled the quilt up to her neck. He yanked it away from her, allowing her naked body to feel the nip in the air. He watched as gooseflesh suddenly appeared over her arms and legs.

"I want to sleep a little more," she whined, grasping the air for the quilt, which he moved down even further out of her reach.

Though her nimble, naked body caused a flurry of unwholesome thoughts, and he would have preferred to rejoin her in bed, he was firm in his resolve. He wouldn't tolerate laziness from himself or from her. He planted a smart slap on her rump and said in a firmer voice, "Up, Susannah. There's work to be done, and it's light outside."

Grumbling nonsensically, she sat up as he stood to his feet. She glared at him before her face softened into a smile. "Good morning, husband."

Her greeting was so sweet that Adam had to stoop to kiss her, which gave her the opportunity to wrap her arms around his neck and pull him closer, trying to bring him back to bed. Instead, he linked one strong arm around her waist and hauled her forward to her feet, where he continued to kiss her. His cock twitched under his trousers, and he knew that if she was cheeky enough to feel him again, he would give away how much he would like to return to bed with her.

Rubbing a hand down her back to her bottom, he smiled to himself when she clenched her cheeks. He doubted she would misbehave so soon after a chastisement. When their lips unlocked, he planted another swat on her bottom. "Get dressed." His voice was husky and riddled with arousal even to his own ears. Susannah heard it too because she gave him a much less sweet and much more mischievous smile before turning away to obey. Adam stuffed his twitching palm into his pocket before he succumbed to the temptation to smack her naughty backside again.

Turning his attention to the door, he examined the hinge while she dressed. He heard the sound of tiny footsteps padding across the floor outside of the room, and Adam realized it had to be Caleb, who obviously had an easier time getting out of bed than his mother. Adam shoved the door and propped it open, deciding that the door would be the first thing he would attend to that morning.

Caleb stood nearby and stared up at him with wide, curious eyes.

"Hello, kid. How'd you sleep?"

Caleb let out a shy giggle and bounded away from him toward the Dutch oven. His mother followed and got to work lighting it, admonishing Caleb to stay away so he wouldn't get burned. Adam noticed that the child didn't mind his mother, and he also noticed that Susannah did nothing about that. Instead, she kept shooing him away, and he kept returning moments later.

The whole scenario bothered Adam. He thought Susannah should do a better job of getting her child to behave. He also felt worried that Caleb's lack of obedience would indeed get him burned eventually, and he could see that Susannah was struggling through the task of cooking breakfast when she so often had to focus attention on her son.

"Caleb, come here," Adam said, hearing the authority in his own voice. Caleb heard it too because his eyes grew wide again. His nervous gaze darted to his mother, who nodded at him encouragingly.

"Go on," she said.

Caleb leaned forward to where Susannah was crouched in front of the oven and whispered something in her ear. She smiled and looked over at Adam. "He's wondering if he should call you 'pa.'"

Adam's heart constricted painfully. He'd never intended on being a father, and suddenly becoming one caused a rush of memories about his deceased siblings to flood his mind. It was overwhelming for him to suddenly have a child, but he quickly realized it had to be just as overwhelming for the lad to suddenly have a father.

Adam smiled at Susannah and then at Caleb. "That would be just fine to call me 'pa', son, seein' as how that's what I am. Now come on over here, please," he repeated.

Caleb walked to him, still looking shy, which was quite different from how he'd acted the previous evening. Adam hoped it wouldn't be long before the boy became comfortable again. He crouched down to meet him at eye level.

Though Adam didn't know much about how to talk to children, he remembered when he was a boy and how important it had made him feel to help out his father, so he took that approach. "I need your help, little man. Do you know where there are some tools around here, like a hammer and nails?"

Caleb's eyes lit up and he nodded. He pressed his small hand into Adam's just like he had done before and pulled him toward a tin box on the bookshelf. Adam shot Susannah a wink, and she smiled gratefully at him. It seemed she understood that one of Adam's motives for getting Caleb busy was to free her to cook breakfast, and the shining in her eyes told Adam just how much she appreciated it.

Caleb sat cross-legged on the floor, watching Adam in rapt attention as he fixed the door hinge. Adam told him whenever he needed a screw or tool, and Caleb would find it and hand it to him after Adam described it. At the end of the task, when the door had but one piece of wood loose from the frame, Adam hammered a nail nearly the full way in, then waved for Caleb to come closer. He handed the boy the hammer and told him to hit the nail. The boy hammered it home after a few false swings. Adam tousled his hair and praised him. "You fixin' to be a carpenter? I reckon you're a natural."

Caleb beamed at him with a proud smile on his face.

"I think it's you who's the natural, Adam," Susannah said softly. Adam turned to find her wiping away a tear. "Come on over and sit down, you two. Breakfast is ready."

The stool Adam sat on felt unsteady, so he made a mental note to fix that too in a jiffy, hoping it didn't break underneath him during the meal. He observed the sniffling woman spooning eggs onto his plate. She wouldn't meet his eyes. Instead, she turned her back to them and tried to discreetly lift the hem of her apron to dry her tears.

"Why are you sad, Ma?" Caleb asked, his voice sounding concerned and his brows furrowed in worry.

"I'm not, sweetheart," she assured him. "I'm crying because I'm happy." She let out another sob and hiccup.

Caleb's worried look turned into an expression of confusion, which he turned on Adam. "Why is she crying if she's happy?"

Adam shrugged. "Beats me. It's a woman thing, I reckon."

When Susannah continued to sniffle with her back facing them, he sighed. "Quit your caterwauling and sit down, woman." He said it gruffly but with an affectionate note in his tone.

She choked out a laugh and turned around, her eyes rimmed with red. "Everything's good," she said to Caleb as she sat.

Adam mostly agreed that everything was good. One thing that was not good, however, was the meal, but he didn't complain. He was hungry enough that the runniness of the eggs and the burned bacon just barely caught his attention. He would save the discussion about her cooking for another day. He didn't want to criticize her, but he firmly believed that people should do their best at whatever they did. Since it was his wife's job to cook, he would expect her to be good at it. He would also expect Caleb to do well in school when he attended.

Adam knew that to some he seemed demanding, but he never expected more of others than he did of himself. Those who got to know him generally came to appreciate this about him. He wondered if his wife would be one of them.

Chapter Seven

The following weeks were filled with long but happy days for Adam, during which he became acquainted with his new family. He could hardly keep his hands off of Susannah, and it was with great joy that he discovered she didn't want him to. The woman was insatiable. A look from him and a kiss would make her come alive in his arms. She responded to his dominance, becoming hopelessly aroused when he ordered her to bend over, spread her legs, or get on her knees. Delaying her releases or threatening to disallow them drove her wild with anticipation.

Adam knew another man had taken her virtue, and he'd thought that might bother him. He'd fantasized about enlightening a chaste woman about the pleasures to be had in bed, but after bedding Susannah, that fantasy disappeared entirely. In its stead was a far greater desire—to delight often in a woman who wanted to please him as much as he wanted to please her.

Adam also became acquainted with the foreman, the cowhands, and the inner workings of the ranch. The work that needed to be done was extensive. While Timothy wasn't a bad man, he hadn't run the place as a foreman should, with efficiency and authority, and age had made him slow and complacent when it came to being a boss. Two of the cowhands were obviously lazy, and the other four needed clear instructions on what to do, since they seemed to be wholly without initiative.

When Adam had arrived at the range with Timothy on the first day, he'd found all the hands idling about. He'd quickly determined that three of the men should be riding the perimeter and fixing the fences, and the rest should be driving the cattle to greener pastures and branding the thirty head of cattle that were without marking. Within a few days, Adam had assumed leadership of everything that was previously in Timothy's purview and had all the men under orders, working for their pay. He was aware of the resentment emanating from the men who hitherto had been content with spending their days in leisure. They grumbled amongst each other within his range of hearing. The bellyaching he would allow for a spell, but laziness he would not.

He understood what it must feel like to suddenly have a demanding boss, when they had been without any instructions for so long. He was also keenly aware that he had not exactly earned his position as head of the ranch. He had responded to an ad in the paper and he'd gotten lucky. Still, he knew what it took to keep a ranch profitable, and he was going to see to it that it succeeded. Now that he owned a fertile ranch with the boundaries clearly spelled out in the deed, there was no reason why he couldn't ensure its success.

In addition to idleness, another vice he wouldn't tolerate was impulsive spending, which he came to learn was a vice his new wife possessed. As he became acquainted with the ledger book, he noticed that there were large amounts of money the ranch earned that were unaccounted for. Returning home after a long day of driving cattle, he found a stack of calico, ribbons, and sweets next to the doorway, and he put two and two together.

He hung his Stetson on a hook next to the door and placed his hands on his hips. "Susannah!" he called, his displeasure with her apparent in the way he said her name.

His wife entered the sitting room and scurried over to give him a kiss. He returned the kiss, but then returned to the matter on his mind. Waving a hand at the stack of goods, he said, "What is this? Are you fixin' to make all new clothes and chow on candy every day for a month?"

It was the first time since the day of their meeting that Adam had scolded her. After living in a state of perpetual marital bliss, he wasn't surprised to see the shock on his wife's face. He was, however, surprised by the conversation that followed.

Susannah stepped back and scowled. "I like to wear nice clothes. My dresses are threadbare and faded, and Caleb needs new trousers for when he starts school in a few months."

Adam swept his gaze over her. The dress she was wearing looked perfectly suitable to him. In fact, he thought she looked downright stunning. The dress was a bright yellow color that wasn't faded in the least. Even if the fabric was worn out, he didn't see why she needed all the new material, which would make at least ten dresses. He frowned and said just that, then added, "This is reckless spending. You need to return half of the fabric and take back all but one bag of candy. The ranch is doing fine right now, but we need to save for a rainy day."

As far as Adam was concerned, this was a fair request for a husband to make of his wife. He was responsible for the family's finances, and if he thought the money wasn't being used wisely, he felt he had every right to fix that.

Susannah placed her hands on her hips, matching his stance. "We have plenty of money to spend a little extra."

He scowled down at her. "How would you know? You aren't involved in the accounting."

Skirting the question, she said, "My pa would have let me buy all this and not said a word. And he was obviously involved in the accounting like you are."

"Well, your pa ain't here, Susannah, and I'd wager that this was one of the reasons he set things up how he did in the will. He knew you'd need a man to see to the business affairs."

The implication that her father didn't trust her to manage the ranch on her own was a sore subject, evidenced in the red anger creeping into her cheeks and around her ears. "You have some nerve, acting like it's within your right to order me not to spend my own money."

Adam felt his jaw clench. He didn't like the direction the conversation was going, but he wasn't going to back down. "I'm only asking you to show some moderation, not stop spending altogether."

"That's not fair," she said, her voice rising with fury. "He was my father, it was my land to inherit! It's my ranch, my money. And your asking sounds a lot like ordering, which you have no right to do."

Adam drew a deep breath as he felt his temper rise. He decided it was best to abandon the conversation for the time being, so he walked away from her to the bedroom. He needed to change out of his dusty work clothes and collect his thoughts. He felt tired, irritable, and now he was angry with his wife.

Susannah was still rarin' to fight, so she followed him into the bedroom. "I know the law says the money belongs to you, but don't forget where this money came from and how you acquired it. You didn't have two nickels to rub together before you met me," she growled.

It was a low blow. Adam didn't respond right away. Instead, he concentrated on unbuttoning his dirty shirt and shucking it. Removing a clean shirt from the dresser, he finally spoke. "You're right, I was a poor man before I married you. I lost my ranch, and that means I know what a ranch headed toward failure looks like. Lemme tell you something, Susannah, it wasn't lookin' good around here. Your foreman was acting soft and didn't notice that the hands needed to feel the sharp end of a cattle prod. You weren't feeding the chickens properly or tendin' to the garden. What you needed was a man to take charge, and that man, for better or worse, is me."

She blinked and stared at him, looking unsure about how to respond.

Gritting his teeth, he continued, "So tell me, is this how it's going to be? Are you going to remind me for the rest of our lives together that I came with nothing and everything rightfully belongs to you?"

Her eyes widened and her mouth rounded into an O. He watched as fury faded from her eyes, replaced by the beginnings of regret. "That's not what I meant, Adam."

He folded his arms in front of his chest. "No? That's what it sounded like to me."

She looked down and fiddled with the lace on her sleeves. "I just meant that…" Her voice trailed off. She looked up at him sorrowfully. "I'm sorry. I don't really think that. It's your money too."

"Look, Susannah, I told you why I lost the ranch I inherited from my father. At that time, I only had myself to worry about. Now suddenly you and Caleb are my responsibility. God forbid the ranch starts to head south for some reason, I want to know you won't starve. Saving money is important, and I'm going to insist on it."

She rushed over. She placed her hand on his chest and looked up at him. "I understand, Adam, and I thank you for thinking about the future. I just—I'm used to being able to buy what I like. How you run things, it's not what I was expecting. I wasn't expecting you to run things at all."

Adam stiffened. He didn't return her touch. Scowling down at her, he said, "Take back the materials, and from now on, you ask my permission before you buy something other than the basics."

"Yes, sir," she said, sounding near tears. She took a step back and stared at the floor.

He walked past her to exit the room.

"Adam…" she said beseechingly.

He stopped at the doorway and half-turned to look at her. His jaw ached from clenching it in anger, and he knew he looked as angry as he felt. She should have let him go. "Yes, Susannah?" he said more sharply that he should have.

She visibly winced at the reproachful sound of his voice. "I shouldn't have said that. Forgive me?"

He reckoned a better man would have offered her his forgiveness, but he felt no desire to accept her apology in that moment. She had dealt him a low blow by reminding him that he was a poor man benefiting from her riches, and it was taking everything in his power not to hurt her back with his words. He kept himself from lashing out at her, but that was all he was able to do. He could not offer her a kind word after her apology. Instead he said, "I'll be out on the porch. Call me when supper is ready."

Tears flooded her eyes. "Yes, Adam," she said, her voice barely above a whisper.

That evening when they lay in bed, Adam did not make love to her for the first time since they'd been married. Her words filled his mind, and he knew one of the reasons they affected him so much was that they were partly true. He hadn't earned the ranch. It had been handed to him, and it made him feel wretched. How was he to be a good leader of his newly acquired family, when his wife knew that before he met her, he'd possessed little more than a change of duds and high hopes?

A wave of sadness and anger over the ranch he'd lost washed over him. Since arriving in Virginia City, Susannah and Caleb had filled his heart with so much happiness that there wasn't enough room for devastation about the loss of his pa's ranch. With some of that joy shattered, Adam felt the pain of his loss once again. He fell asleep angry, and he woke up the same way.

Chapter Eight

Even though he was not the kind of man she originally wanted, Susannah loved Adam more and more as the days passed. He was firm and disciplined, a good leader, and so many of her worries melted away after he'd come into her life. Knowing he was managing the business affairs in such a way that their little family would be safe and well cared for gave her relief.

But, as was wont to happen more often than she liked, her temper and impulsiveness had made an ugly appearance. In her anger, she had said the very words she suspected would hurt her husband, and she had been right. Instead of feeling victorious, she'd felt instantly regretful.

Things were not the same in the days that followed. Adam was distant. He carried on with the habits of each day, but he no longer was warm toward her—only polite. He still kissed her hello and goodbye, but those gestures seemed more out of obligation than any meaningful sentiment. He didn't make love to her, and she missed that. She wanted him to go back to handling her in the strong, tender way he had in the beginning, before she'd challenged his leadership by insulting him. She hoped every day that he would forgive her, but she couldn't see any softening in his interactions with her.

Though deeply saddened that she had damaged their relationship, she was grateful to notice that her words didn't seem to have any negative repercussions when it came to Adam's relationship with Caleb. From day one, Adam and her son had gotten along, and they only continued to bond. Caleb followed Adam around often, asking questions about whatever he was doing. Adam answered him patiently, taking the time to explain. Whenever he would ask the boy to do something, Caleb was quick to obey. The boy reserved his rebellion for when Adam was at the range, and Susannah wondered if he would ever act up in front of his new pa. She also wondered how Adam would react if he did.

One evening the three of them were relaxing near the dim light of the lamp. Susannah rocked back and forth in her chair, which Adam had recently fixed, humming to herself and mending the curtains. Adam sat on a stool nearer to the light, while Caleb sat on the floor next to him and watched him whittle away at some wood.

"What's that, Pa?"

Susannah smiled to herself over Caleb calling him Pa. Even if Adam never warmed to her again, she would be grateful that he was in their lives due to his kindness toward her son.

Adam stopped whittling and held up his project so that the boy could see it. About halfway done, the sculpture was shaped into a horse's head with a long flowing mane.

"Oh! It's a horse," Caleb exclaimed, clapping his hands together and grinning.

"Almost," Adam said with a smile, and resumed his task of whittling the horse's withers.

"Can I try? I want to know how to make horses out of wood." He leaned forward and rested his head against Adam's leg.

"I'll give you a lesson tomorrow in the full light of day, how about that?" Adam said. "I'll have to show you how to use the knife the right way so you don't cut yourself."

One thing Caleb did not like doing was waiting, but he didn't argue. He yawned and appeared to be struggling to keep his eyes open.

Adam bounced his knee to jostle Caleb's head. "Time for bed, little man."

Caleb's posture became straighter as though to convince himself and Adam that he wasn't sleepy. "I don't want to go to bed," he whined.

Adam set aside the whittling project and looked down at him with a kind look in his eyes. "Sometimes we have to do things we don't wanna do, son. That's just the way life is." He took hold of the boy's arms and pulled him to his feet. "Be a good lad and get to bed, yeah?"

"Fine," he said sullenly.

"Not 'fine'," Adam admonished, his voice taking on a hint of sternness. "It's either 'yes, sir' or 'yes, Pa'."

Caleb frowned at him for a moment but then mumbled, "Yes, sir."

"Thank you. Go say goodnight to your ma."

Caleb scurried over to Susannah, who gave him a big kiss on his cheek. She was very proud of him for being so good and only resisting Adam's order once.

"Mama, can I have a peppermint stick before I go to bed?"

Usually she would have said yes, but Adam's success at putting his foot down fueled her courage, and she thought she might piggyback off his authority. "No, sweetheart. You already had one after supper."

"But, Ma! I want one," he exclaimed. "That's not fair, you always give me a sweet before bed."

"Not this time. Go on now, Caleb," she said wearily.

"I'm getting a peppermint, and then I'll go to bed," he declared and stomped in the direction of the kitchen.

Susannah looked at Adam and shrugged. She decided it was better to let him have his candy as opposed to becoming victim to one of his tantrums.

Adam narrowed his eyes at her and shook his head with disapproval. When she resumed mending, he let out a sigh of annoyance she knew was directed at her. Adam stood and strode to Caleb, who had already picked out a piece of candy from the brown paper bag on the table. Taking his arm, he removed the candy from his hand and dragged him toward his room, while Caleb wailed the entire time and refused to use his legs to walk.

"Not only are you not getting candy tonight, young man, you won't be getting any for the rest of the week for disobeying your ma." Adam opened the door to his bedroom and tugged him along inside.

The sound of Caleb's wails increased such that one would have thought the world was ending. Susannah followed them into the room, worried about what would happen next.

Adam plopped the boy on the bed and held a finger in front of his tear-streaked face. "When you're bad, there are consequences. You can cry all you like, but it's not gonna change anything." He placed his hands on his hips and glared down at the boy without sympathy or attempt to comfort him, waiting for his crying to stop.

Eventually, Caleb's cries turned into hiccups, and he rubbed his eyes. He looked at Adam with a wounded expression on his face, likely surprised at having been scolded by his new pa, who had up until that point been nothing but mild toward him. His lower lip quivered and he sniffled, looking like he would burst into tears again at any moment. Adam fished out a handkerchief from his pocket and held it over his nose. "Blow," he instructed.

After Caleb blew a few times, he asked in a small, wobbling voice, "Are you still mad at me, Pa?"

Adam shook his head. "I'm not mad at all. But I want you to behave yourself better in the future. You must mind your ma and me, ya hear? Next time you disobey or throw a tantrum I'll punish you."

Caleb stared at him, still looking hurt and now a little surprised. "You will?"

"If you misbehave again, yes," Adam confirmed.

"I'll be good," he said, sounding subdued. He swiped the back of his hand under his eyes to wipe away the last of his tears.

"Lie down and go to sleep, son," Adam said in a gentler voice.

Caleb nodded and climbed up to rest his head on his pillow. Adam pulled up the quilt and tucked it around him.

"Can I have a sweet tomorrow?"

"Of course not," Adam exclaimed. "What did I just tell you?"

"You said I couldn't have any for the rest of the week, but I thought you might change your mind, seein' as how you're not mad at me."

Adam snorted a laugh. "Nice try. You'll find I don't often change my mind, Caleb. Go to sleep." He tousled his hair and then left the room.

When Susannah joined him a moment later, he scowled at her. "If I find out you've given him candy while I'm at the range, I'll turn you both over my knee."

Surprised, she said, "I won't do that, Adam. I wouldn't go behind your back like that."

He raised a brow. "Sure about that? You're way too soft on the boy."

Her temper flared at his criticism. "Are you saying I'm a bad mother?"

"Oh, for Pete's sake," he said, sounding exasperated. "No, I just think you need to be a little firmer and not spoil him. You notice he doesn't try to get away with that tomfoolery with me. That's because he can tell it won't work."

Susannah scowled, offended by the implication that she was doing something wrong. Adam had no idea how stubborn Caleb was and how loath she was to correct him. It was true that she spoiled him, but she hadn't been able to give him a complete family. Until Adam came along, she felt like she had to make up for that in some way, and spoiling him a little seemed to be the best way in which to do it.

"You have no right! He's my son, not yours. You've only been around for a short time and you don't know—"

Adam held a finger to her lips. "Hush. You're saying something you'll regret just like last time I dared to act like I have some say in how things work around here."

His warm finger pressed against her mouth, plus the truth of his words, caused the fight to leave her. She stared into his narrowed eyes and felt her own eyes soften with submission. He noticed it too because he moved his finger away and cupped her cheek, brushing over it with the pad of his thumb. "Good girl."

His tender, dominant approval gave her a surge of hope. The Adam she'd first met seemed to be back, standing in front of her. He curled his hand around the nape of her neck and pulled her head closer before he pressed his lips to hers. Her hands fell off her hips and suddenly her whole body was wrapped up in his embrace. Her palms found his shoulder blades, and his chest pressed against her breasts. Her tummy fluttered at his strong touch, which she'd been missing since she'd insulted him so terribly.

When he released her lips, he smiled at her. "My little kitten has sharp claws."

She smiled sheepishly. "I have a hot temper. It's always been a weakness."

"Your hot temper will lead to a hot bottom next time, darlin'."

She stared into his eyes, sobering. "I would prefer to be spanked every day than to bear one more day of you being cold toward me."

"I'll remember that." He gave her another quick kiss. "My ma was like you are with Caleb—very soft and tolerant. I would cause all kinds of ruckus and she would only smile at me or beg me to settle down."

"You caused a ruckus?" Susannah asked, her face softening into a smile. "I can't even picture you being rowdy. You're always so calm and in control."

Adam chuckled. "I suppose I turned out that way because of my pa. He was not so tolerant of misbehavior, and he was also slow to praise. I spent my whole life tryin' to make my father proud of me. With my ma, I always knew I had her approval."

"I'm sure both of them were proud of you."

Adam smiled. "They were good parents. I wish you could have met them."

"And I wish you could have met my pa. I always felt like he was proud of me, until the end. I really disappointed him." Susannah felt the sharp pangs of regret over how her father had died still ashamed of her.

"Hey," Adam said softly, smoothing a lock of her hair behind her ear. "Your pa wanted what was best for you. He would've come around if he'd lived longer."

She shook her head slightly. "I doubt it. He had a few years to come around after I had Caleb, but he never did. I saw the disappointment in his eyes until his very last day."

Adam frowned and rubbed his chin. "I don't rightly understand your pa. You were young and full of normal desire, and your only sin was trusting a scoundrel. It's not your fault, sweetheart. You didn't deserve to be shamed by everyone in such a way."

She gazed into his eyes, feeling so touched by his words she could hardly choke hers out. "You don't think less of me. You don't think I'm a whore like all the townsfolk do."

"Of course not!" he exclaimed.

"I'm so glad. I want you to think well of me."

"I do, honey." A familiar twinkle crept into his eyes, a look she had desperately missed seeing as of late. "Unless you want me to think of you as a whore. I like you being my little wanton harlot in the bedroom."

She blushed, loving his possessive words and the memories of their bedroom activities. "I like being your whore too."

Adam laughed briefly, but then sobered again. "Back to the subject of a father's disappointment, I don't know much about being a father, but I do remember how much it hurt when I disappointed my own. I know I wouldn't want Caleb to feel my disapproval for long. It's better to be disciplined and then forgiven."

"I agree, and I'm glad you're here. He needs a father," she whispered.

"And you need a husband," he said with a sigh. "One who doesn't disapprove of you. I'm sorry for how

I've acted toward you these last few days. It wasn't right of me."

She shook her head and looked down at the floor. "It was my fault. I shouldn't have said what I did."

"No, you shouldn't have," Adam agreed, taking her into his arms once again. "But it was my duty to set you straight instead of giving you the cold shoulder. I didn't realize it would be such a sore subject, but what you said reminded me that I hadn't earned this ranch, and it reminded me of the ranch I lost. The ranch in Amarillo was my father's legacy, and then I lost it."

She blinked, chasing away the tears that were forming, and shook her head emphatically. "Maybe you didn't earn this ranch in the traditional way, Adam, but we couldn't live without you now. Just you being here, you've already made so many good changes I didn't even realize needed changing. You mentioned only a few of them. You're a good man. This ranch needs you, and me and Caleb do too."

His lips spread into a sly grin. "It's nice to hear you say that, darlin'. I'm not all good though. I want to do some very wicked things to you right now." He took her hand in his and led her to their bedroom. Once inside, he closed the door, latched it, and then kissed her. Their passion grew, and he reached around to unbutton the first of many buttons on her dress, starting with the one at the nape of her neck.

"So, you want to replace this dress with a new one, hmm?" he muttered, remembering the argument that had led to such a rift between them.

"No, I don't need to, Adam," she said, her voice nearly breathless. "I don't need new dresses."

He loved how she was responding to him, and it caused a surge of dominance to course through his veins. "That's not what you told me. 'Threadbare' was the word you used, I believe. Were you fibbing, kitten?" He asked the question with a warning note in his voice that he knew would make her feel naughty. He unbuttoned the next button slowly, causing her to moan with impatience and reach around to assist with undressing.

"Hands at your side," he said in a clipped voice.

She obeyed with a little squeak that made him bite back a smile. She acted like she wanted control, but her actions in that moment made her true desires clear to him.

He suddenly spun her around so that her back faced him. He grasped the fabric of the dress and with both hands ripped it apart, revealing her pale, naked back. She gasped, but he continued to undress her forcefully, tearing off the rest of the material, popping off the frock's buttons. He was ready to take what was his.

"Adam…," she gasped.

"You wanted a new dress, darlin'," he snarled against her neck, then bit her a little harder than what was comfortable. She let out a quiet whine of protest. He pressed his hand against her back at her shoulder blades and pushed her to her stomach on the bed.

Adam stood to her side and curled his hand around the nape of her neck. Pinning her in place, he ran his other hand down the length of her back lightly. He landed a hard smack on her bottom and watched as his handprint bloomed over her cheek. He smacked her again on her other cheek and continued, finding a steady rhythm. Susannah remained in place, accepting the swats with small gasps and whimpers.

He continued spanking her, hard but slowly, pausing a moment after each spank to allow the full pain of it sink in. "You know you've earned this, don't you? I can tell because you're being a good girl and accepting it."

"Yes, sir," she said, her voice soft and submissive. "Thank you."

He felt his cock lengthening in his trousers. This sight of her naked and pinned, accepting discipline with nary a word of complaint, and in fact thanking him, fed his desire to claim and dominate her. "You'll accept my leadership in the future. I've shown you I'm capable of taking care of this family and the ranch, and that's what you need, isn't it?"

"Yes, Adam. I need it so much," she choked out.

He spanked her again. "And the next time I make a decision you don't like, what will you do?"

"I'll obey you," she moaned.

"You certainly will. And what about that temper of yours?"

"I'll keep it in check."

He smacked her hard twice. "You'd better, young lady, if you like sitting occasionally."

He circled behind her. After setting his cock free, he grasped her hips and dragged her ass to his stomach. Her knees boosted her on the bed, but her head still touched the quilt. He reached around and slid his fingers along her slit, groaning when he found her womanhood slick with desire. "You're so wet for me, kitten," he said, his voice husky. "Do you think I should let you come?"

"Oh, please, Adam," she gasped.

He wasn't gentle. He shoved his cock inside her to the hilt, filling her and claiming her body as his. She let out whimpers as he fucked her hard, smacking her ass and grabbing her fleshy warm cheeks. This was not a lovemaking session. There would be plenty of time for those in the future. This was a statement, a reinforcement of their relationship, and he could tell she needed it as much as he did.

A particularly hard thrust caused her to cry out loudly, so Adam reached around and clamped his hand firmly over her mouth. "Hush, woman. The whole world doesn't need to know you're getting your naughty little cunt fucked."

She moaned and tried to speak behind his hand, but he kept it in place while he continued to thrust his cock in and out of her wet pussy. Suddenly she bit one of his fingers, not enough to draw blood, but enough to cause his reflexes to jerk his hand away from her mouth. He slowed his movements.

"You bit me," he said, both amused and a little surprised.

"Maybe," came the cheeky response.

He laughed and pulled out of her.

She snarled in protest. "What are you doing?"

In answer to her question, he pressed her hips down to the bed again and spanked her hard and fast, over and over. When she screamed after the fifth stroke of his punishing hand, he shoved her face into the quilt. "I told you to muffle that racket," he growled. "If you don't, I'll put you straight to bed after this spanking. No release."

She wailed, sounding dismayed at the threat.

"You're going to learn restraint and self-discipline, woman, or you're going to be restrained and disciplined by me. You got that?"

"Yes!" came her muffled response. She buried her screams as he painted her every inch of her bottom a crimson shade of red, spanking so hard that her mound crushed against the quilt with every swat.

He could hear sheer pleasure in her dim cries and knew he was giving her exactly what she needed. Biting him was a test, a physical representation of her temper, and she needed to know he would respond in this way, not in the terrible way he had before.

He saw her stiffen and shudder, and realized with no small amount of awe that she was about to orgasm just from the spanking. "Bad little kitten!" He stopped spanking, grabbed her hips, and sank into her. A few thrusts later her back arched and she stiffened again, her tight cunt clenching over and over around his cock, driving him so crazy that he came right as she was settling down.

He collapsed on top of her, his entire large body pinning her much smaller body in place while he caught his breath. She squirmed. "You're squashing me, Adam."

Adam rolled over onto his back, freeing her. She remained on her stomach and stared at him. Her lips curled into a mischievous smile. "You speak very crudely when you make love to me."

He propped himself up by an elbow and ran his fingers through her mussed hair, a loving touch that differed sharply from the punishing sex. "That wasn't making love, kitten. That was fucking my little whore."

She burst out laughing, and he joined her. It was one of those perfect moments in life. They were again at peace with each other, Caleb was safe in his bed, and the business was thriving. Adam sighed with contentment and closed his eyes. As he drifted to sleep, he reflected on how different his Susannah was from the type of woman he used to dream about. He let out a prayer of thanks, grateful he'd been given exactly what he didn't know he wanted.

Chapter Nine

The summer months were fruitful. Susannah watched with amazement as the stock of cattle multiplied, the chickens laid tasty eggs every day, the vegetable garden flourished, and two new colts were birthed. During this time, Adam showed Caleb how to perform a variety of outside chores like gathering eggs and weeding the garden.

Susannah could see that her son was eager to please his new pa because he didn't fuss and instead took on every new chore cheerfully. Soon school would be filling his days, but until then, Adam kept him occupied in a way she never had. It had never occurred to her that she should teach him practical skills, as her father had never required her to do chores as a child.

Adam also began giving Caleb riding lessons on the old mare Liza. The horse was patient and didn't spook easily, and Caleb learned quickly. Occasionally Adam would offer him a word or two of praise, and Susannah noticed that her son was so eager to make Adam proud that his tantrums had all but disappeared.

Sometimes it was hard for her to watch Adam pushing her son to try harder and do better, often sternly and without compromise. Caleb was not used to being pushed so hard, and Adam seemed too demanding. In the back of her mind, however, a voice told her that this was what a father did to make a boy a man. She knew that his influence would serve Caleb well, so she stayed silent.

Susannah was not spared from Adam's high expectations and insistence on proper behavior. His criticism irritated her, especially when he didn't seem to notice everything she was doing right, and instead only pointed out her shortcomings. She made the mistake of napping one too many times in his presence, which he considered unacceptable unless taken ill.

On a hot afternoon, she woke up to the sound of her name being spoken sharply, which immediately put her in a bad mood. She rubbed her eyes and found Adam standing by the bed with his hands on his hips, scowling down at her. "What in tarnation are you doing sleeping? I've been working all day, I'm half-starved, and you haven't cooked anything."

She groaned and rolled out of bed. "I lost track of the time. I'll cook something now."

"Are you not feeling well?" he asked. "This is the third time I've found you sleeping in the middle of the day." His voice had softened a bit, and she knew that he would stop being cross with her if she said she didn't feel well, but she didn't want to lie to him. She felt overwhelmed at times, but she didn't feel ill.

"I'm fine," she grunted.

Perhaps if she had apologized, he would have let it go at that, but her response only seemed to make him grumpier. "I don't tolerate laziness from my hands, so I'm certainly not going to tolerate it from my wife," he said, following her into the kitchen. He stood near her with his arms folded in front of his chest as she lit the oven.

Caleb joined them. "I'm hungry," he whined.

Susannah felt a pang of regret when she looked down at her son. He appeared dirty, and she hadn't fed him a meal since breakfast, instead allowing him to eat sweets whenever he wanted. It was past his week-long restriction of no candy, but Susannah knew she should have provided him with something healthier throughout the day.

She opened the keep and retrieved the potatoes and carrots they'd recently harvested from the garden. "This won't take long," she mumbled. Turning her back on the two hungry boys in the kitchen, she peeled the potatoes as quickly as she could. She hated cooking. In fact, she hated chores of every kind, and she'd never quite gotten used to doing them after the cook and maid had quit.

"Caleb, go play in your room," Adam ordered.

"But I didn't do anything wrong," the boy protested. "Why do I have to leave?"

"Because I need to talk to your ma privately. I'll call you when supper is ready."

Caleb let out an affronted sigh and trudged to his room looking very unhappy.

He wasn't nearly as unhappy as Susannah. Her spirits sank lower, knowing Adam had ordered him away to scold her.

They watched Caleb disappear into the bedroom. Adam turned his attention to her once again. "If you were one of my hands, I'd dock your pay. Once is understandable, but twice is unacceptable, and three times is cause for discipline."

She resumed peeling the potatoes, slicing with force. "Well, good thing I'm not one of your hands," she retorted snottily.

He let out a low whistle. "Land's sake, woman. If you want a spanking, there are easier ways of getting one."

"You're being unfair! I'm your wife, and you're not my boss."

"Only one part of that is true," he said, a modicum of humor in his voice.

His amusement only made her angrier. She spun to face him. "Look, I'm not used to cooking and housekeeping, all right? I didn't do any of it growing up because my father had servants. I'm doing my best."

He studied her and raised an eyebrow slowly. "Are you?" His gaze traveled around the messy room. Unwashed clothes hung over his armchair, Caleb's blocks were scattered around the fireplace, and she hadn't refilled the firewood bin with the wood he'd chopped the other day. "This is your best?"

She took in a sharp breath. He had just managed to genuinely hurt her feelings. "I can't believe you said that. You are so… mean!"

"Honey, I'm not trying to be mean," he said with a sigh. "Let's discuss this after supper. I'm hungry and irritable, and I'm afraid I'm about to lose my temper with you, which I don't want to do."

"Thank you. How very thoughtful," she said sarcastically, and turned back around to continue her task. He gave her bottom a smack that was more playful than punishing, and it didn't hurt a bit through all the layers of skirts, but it made her growl. She looked over her shoulder and glared at his back as he walked away from her to the sitting room. Honestly! She felt angry at having been criticized. He didn't know how much work it was cooking and cleaning every day, not to mention running after a rambunctious child. So *what* if she took a nap every once in a while? Why did he have to be so hard on her?

Conversation was absent during the meal. Susannah stewed in her anger and hurt feelings while Adam mopped his plate, appearing like he hadn't eaten for weeks. Caleb seemed to sense the tension in the air and wisely refrained from jabbering like he normally did during supper.

The food didn't taste good. She hadn't bothered to add seasoning because Adam had treated her unfairly and she felt justified in giving him nothing but the minimum. She wouldn't let him starve, but that was the extent of her benevolence.

After supper, she scrubbed the dishes as Adam sat in the sitting room with Caleb, lending him his whittling knife and supervising him as he made attempts to shape wood into a dog. Normally, this kind of evening would have caused Susannah's heart to fill with love and contentedness, but on that evening, she felt resentful. They were enjoying themselves, and she was stuck in the kitchen.

When she finished cleaning up and joined them in the sitting room, she plopped down on the rocking chair, feeling tired and upset. That was when Adam told Caleb it was time for bed. She leaned back in the chair and closed her eyes, hoping that Adam would make no further mention of her work.

"Susannah," he said when they were alone, "you were telling me about how you're not used to working and how what I'm seeing is the best you can do."

She opened her eyes and glared at him. She hated how he made her sound spoiled and weak. "I work hard. You don't appreciate me."

"Poppycock. I appreciate you a whole lot. You're the best thing to ever happen to me, so let's get that straight before we continue this chinwag."

It was a nice thing for him to say, and some of her hurt feelings drained out of her. "It doesn't seem like you appreciate me, Adam. You're too hard on me," she pouted.

He frowned. "I would agree I'm hard on you. I know I expect a lot from you and everyone else around me."

"Good. I'm glad you admit it," she grumped.

"I do not think I'm *too* hard on you, though. It's reasonable for me to expect a meal on the table when I get home, is it not? When I get home I'm hungry and want to enjoy supper with my family."

She huffed, knowing it wasn't too much for him to ask but not wanting to admit it.

"I also think you need to learn to cook better. There was no seasoning at all in tonight's supper."

Her anger returned in spades. She stood to her feet. "I did that on purpose! I'm mad at you. You don't deserve flavorful food."

Surprise lit his eyes briefly, followed by a wicked flash of humor. "I see." Clearing his throat, he stood as well. "That was hardly necessary, darlin'. Even with seasoning, your cooking is awful. You needn't punish me further."

She could hardly believe her ears. Her jaw dropped and she stared at him for a moment before she found her voice. "How *dare* you?"

He burst out laughing and held open his arms. "Come here, darlin'."

She shook her head. "You think I want you to hug me after what you just said?"

"Whether you want it or not, I'm telling you to come here," he said with a hint of sternness under the humor, which compelled Susannah to obey.

Exasperated, she walked forward into his open arms. As soon as she buried her face in his chest and he wrapped his arms around her, she felt better.

"You know I love you, right?" he asked, running his hand over her head and raking his fingers through the hair cascading down her back.

It was the first time he'd said the words, and hearing them caused her to feel warm and happy inside, despite having felt angry not two shakes prior. "I love you too."

He squeezed her tighter. "How about if I hire someone to help you with the chores for a while? Would you like that?"

She lifted her head so she could look into his eyes. "Really?"

"Of course. I have cowhands to help me. I don't see why you shouldn't have someone around to help you. We can afford it."

She smiled at him. "Thank you, Adam. I would appreciate that."

"You may choose whoever you like on one condition."

"What?"

"She has to be a good cook, and she has to be willing to teach you everything she knows."

Susannah grunted. "You're insufferable. My cooking isn't that bad. Caleb likes it."

His lips twitched. "The poor boy doesn't know what he's missing out on."

She rolled her eyes. "I'll find someone who can teach me all about cooking so that my husband stops saying mean things."

"Excellent. I'm glad that's settled." He bent and kissed her pouting mouth. "One more thing."

"What?"

"I'm letting it slide this time, but if you ever act like a petulant child again when I make an observation or insist that you try harder, I'm going to tan your hide. That clear?"

She gulped and stared into his eyes, which had turned serious and showed he would make good on his threat. "But it hurts my feelings when you criticize me, Adam."

"If I hurt your feelings, you can tell me that without throwing a fit. You need to be able to accept criticism. It doesn't mean I don't appreciate you."

Susannah didn't respond, so he continued. "And you have the right to tell me if I'm not doing something up to snuff too."

"But you do everything perfectly. It's not fair."

He chuckled. "I'm glad you think so, but I went through a fair share of criticism while learning how to run a ranch. It's not pleasant, but it's necessary."

Susannah wrapped her arms around him and pressed her head against his chest. "Will you say those words again about how you feel?"

He enclosed her body in his arms. "Which words, darlin'? The words about me loving you?"

"Mm hmm."

"I love you," he said, then added, "even though you can't cook a lick."

She groaned and rolled her eyes as she felt his body shaking in silent laughter against her.

Chapter Ten

Susannah acquired the services of a woman named Martha. A well-known and revered presence in Virginia City, Martha led the women's quilting conventions and hosted the cake-baking meetings. Susannah hadn't ever been invited to these events, but the older woman had always been kind to her, which was why Susannah chose to ask her for help. Martha agreed and traveled the two miles to their cabin every other day to assist with the chores. She knew her way around the kitchen, and Susannah learned eagerly, albeit slowly.

"I'm glad you found yourself a husband, dearie," she mentioned on the first day she came to assist. "Talk in the town has settled down—you know, about you bein' a loose woman and all."

Martha's frank words stung, for they were a painful reminder of her reputation. The closer the time came to when she would send Caleb to school, the more she fretted over it. She wouldn't be able to bear it if children treated him badly because of her.

Adam never brought up her reputation in conversation, and he always treated her with respect. But Susannah wanted more than that. She wanted him to praise her, to prove to her that he did not think less of her like so many others did. She didn't spend much time analyzing her need for Adam's approval, though it did cross her mind that she was trying to heal the hurt her father had caused by shaming her for having relations as an unmarried woman.

Like his father before him, Adam was slow to praise, which was difficult enough for her, but when she noticed that it was only on the days when Martha directly assisted her in cooking that Adam mentioned enjoying the meal, she grew increasingly offended.

At supper one evening, Adam looked weary after twelve hours of driving cattle to greener pastures. He wasn't in the mood to talk, let alone argue, and she knew it would be wise to keep her mouth shut. But when he asked her to pass the salt, her temper flared and she couldn't resist speaking up.

"You never ask for salt when Martha cooks," she said, grabbing the shaker and setting it down in front of him with a thud. "Is my cooking not seasoned enough as is for you?"

Adam slowly scattered salt over his roast. Without looking up, he said quietly, "Stop it, Susannah."

"Stop what?" she said, her voice gaining volume and heat. "Stop noticing that you only compliment Martha's cooking?"

He set the salt down next to his plate and glanced at Caleb, who was looking down at his plate. "I didn't know I was doing that," Adam sighed, turning his tired gaze to her. "I don't even know which days Martha is here."

"Well, let me tell you. She's here on the days you say something nice about supper. And on the days when she's not here, you ask me to pass the salt." She dropped her napkin on the table and stood. She stormed to their room and slammed the door behind her, after which she paced the small space, furious with Adam for not appreciating her and furious with herself for not being able to garner a single word of praise from him.

She knew she was being ridiculous, but that didn't stop hot tears from welling up in her eyes. She tried so hard to please him, and it still wasn't good enough. The least he could say was thank you, but those words had never passed through his lips.

Susannah plopped on the bed and stared at her hands, feeling sorry for herself for quite some time. As her anger waned, she realized that she had never thanked him either, for all his hard work around the ranch and at the cabin. Just the other day he had replaced a floorboard in Caleb's room. Though she'd felt thankful, she hadn't expressed it. She groaned out loud. Why did she always let her temper get the better of her? She needed to apologize. It wasn't his fault that he liked Martha's cooking better.

She had just about built up the courage to return to the table to say she was sorry, when Adam entered the room. Before she could say a word, he had grabbed her arm firmly and pulled her to her feet. "I warned you what would happen if you acted like a brat again."

"I'm sorry, Adam," she said, dismayed at reading anger all over his face.

"You're about to be a lot sorrier. I've had a long, hard day, and I don't need my wife giving me grief when I get home."

He marched her all the way to the barn. She knew he was going to punish her, and she didn't try to talk her way out of it. She deserved it, and she hoped her acquiescence would make him go easier on her. It was wishful thinking. He didn't seem of the mind to be the least bit lenient. After he'd lit the lamp and hung it on a nail, he pulled out the bench by the wall and centered it in the barn's walkway. Pointing at it, he said, "Lay yourself down lengthwise on your stomach. It's time I dealt with your temper once and for all."

Her insides clenched with anxiety, and she trembled. Though Adam had taken her over his knee before, this time the punishment promised to be harsh and without the comfort of his body close to hers.

She lay down on the bench awkwardly and with trepidation. The bench was double the width of her body, but her feet dangled off one side, and her head dropped over the other edge.

"Hold on to the legs of the bench," he instructed, his voice hard as steel.

She wrapped a hand around each of the bench's legs and squeezed her eyes shut as he bared her bottom for punishment. It felt humiliating. Though they were the only people in the barn, she felt like the horses and milk cows were watching her as entertainment. First, he lifted each skirt and positioned the fabric on her back. With a tug at the ribbon of her drawers, they loosened around her. His hand slid under her belly and lifted her hips up briefly so that he could slide the material down her legs. His touch on her stomach was gentle and reminded her of how he touched her when they made love. A tickle of strange pleasure intermingled with her growing anxiety. Her drawers remained on her legs, just above her knees, which somehow made her feel even more vulnerable and naughty.

The minute that followed was the longest of her life. Cool air wafted over her bare skin, and she could feel her thighs shaking. Adam retrieved a strip of leather used to fasten the stirrup to his saddle. The strap was the length of her forearm after he doubled it.

He dropped the leather over her quivering cheeks, letting the implement of punishment reside there while he spoke. "You're getting fifteen licks. They're going to hurt, and you're not to move from this position until you feel every last one. Do you understand?"

"Oh, Adam, you're scaring me," she cried, hating how harsh he sounded. No sign of his love for her could be detected in his voice, and it made her feel miserable.

A lick of fire across her cheeks made her gasp with alarm. It hurt far worse than she ever could have imagined.

"Do you understand?" he repeated with a raised voice.

"Yes!"

"If you move from this position, I will repeat the lick. Is that also understood?"

She sniffled. "Yes, sir."

He crouched down, twined his fingers in her hair, and lifted her head so he could make eye contact. "You're being punished. You should be a little afraid of punishment because it hurts, but I won't be cruel."

"I know," she sniffled. "I'm sorry, I deserve it."

"Yes, you do," he agreed. "If you had told me how you felt instead of throwing a tantrum and storming away, we wouldn't be here." He stood to his full height. Without further delay, the punishment proceeded.

By the time the fifth brand of pain had tattooed her bottom, she was begging him to stop. "Please, I can't take anymore! I will never behave like that again."

"I hope not," he said, and snapped the leather across her bottom again. "How do you expect Caleb not to throw tantrums when he sees you doing it?" he asked, his voice stern and reprimanding.

It was a rhetorical question, one that caused her to wail in distress as another lash burned across her skin. Before she could prepare herself for the next, he lashed her again, and she screamed and rolled off the bench, unable to bear it.

"Please no more," she said, sobbing and clutching her hot cheeks as she knelt next to the bench.

"Get back into position," he said with a raised voice, harsh in its disapproval. She hated how angry he sounded, hated how much she had disappointed him. Her heart ached as much as her bottom, and she longed for nothing more than for him to be pleased with her.

Slowly she placed herself back on the bench, then looked over her shoulder at him. His handsome face was hard, his jaw set in determination. "I told you not to move. That last lick didn't count," he said, and snapped the leather across her skin.

She managed to stay in place but wailed anew. "It hurts so much, I can't bear it. I really can't."

Adam moved the strap to his left hand and ran his right over her cheeks. He rubbed and caressed, and his gentle touch and the moment of respite caused Susannah's sobbing to settle a little.

"You have five more coming," he said, his voice still stern. "I think it's better to finish this now, but I will give you your last strokes tomorrow if you really don't think you can handle more."

"I want you to forgive me," she cried. "I can't bear you being angry."

"I forgive you and I'm not angry," he said. "But I'm still going to finish your punishment, either now or tomorrow. Which is it?"

Susannah stared down at the dimly lit sawdust and straw on the floor of the barn. She felt a tear drop off her face onto the ground. Her bottom throbbed, and five more licks would hurt like the dickens. But the thought of going through this again the next day—all of it, the dread, the humiliation of being bared, the pain— it was too much. She wanted to get it over with.

"Your decision, please," Adam prodded.

"I'll take the rest now," she said in a small voice. "I don't want to dread tomorrow."

"I think that's a wise choice." He placed his hand on the small of her back, holding her in place for the next strokes, which were the hardest of all.

Each lash fell quickly across each cheek in a row, ending with a final stroke on the sensitive underside of her buttocks. She hissed with pain and wiggled her butt in the air, trying to cool the burn.

"Stand up," he instructed, and Susannah did so gingerly. She reached around and rubbed her bare, smarting skin as Adam sat on the bench and tossed aside the strap. "Come lie over my lap."

She obeyed. As she lowered herself over his knees and he pulled her close against his body, she started to relax. She would have preferred to have been over his knees in the first place. Lying over the bench felt particularly punishing, which she suspected was his intent. Now, though, he stroked his hand down each hot cheek and then caressed her sore bottom lightly. It felt so good and comforting that Susannah relaxed completely.

"Better?" he asked, his voice now warm and kind.

She nodded. "That strap hurt so much," she whimpered.

"Mm hmm, I know. I've had the strap before." He continued to caress her in a slow, circular movement up and down each cheek and her upper thighs. "I never want to punish you like that again. Are you going to behave like a grown woman from now on?"

"Yes," she said. "It's just…"

"What, honey?"

"I hope someday you like my cooking. It hurts my feelings that you don't when I try so hard."

He maneuvered her around so that she was sitting on his lap and hugged her to his chest. "Trying is what's important. Like anything else, I imagine it takes practice. Why are you so desperate for my approval?"

She rested her head on his shoulder. She thought about his question for some time until the answer came to her. "I worry I'm a disappointment to you, since I'm not the kind of woman you wanted to marry."

He rubbed a hand down her back. "I thought I knew what I wanted, Susannah, but I didn't. You're it, honey. I hope you'll come to believe that. I don't care what people think about you, and I don't care that you can't cook—only that you try. And I know I'm strict with you, baby, but I think you need that."

He continued to hold her until all her tears had dried and she was dozing off in his arms. She went to sleep that night with a smarting bottom and resolve never to behave like a spoiled child again. Adam was right about how she needed him to be strict with her. It made her feel a little embarrassed, and it really hurt being spanked, but it also made her feel loved, forgiven, and accepted in a way she never had before.

Chapter Eleven

Susannah fretted about sending her little boy to school, not just because of her fear that children would mistreat him, but also because she felt concerned about Caleb's behavior. Adam had helped to prepare him by giving him chores and a routine, but she still worried that the structure of a classroom would be too overwhelming for a boy used to spending his days free to do as he pleased.

She lectured him constantly. The evening before his first day, she said, "Now, Caleb, you're going to walk with Betsy to school tomorrow morning, and you need to walk with her back home. No dawdling. And you must mind what she says."

"Yes, Ma," Caleb mumbled.

Susannah rose from the table and picked up the whiskey on the counter. She poured two fingers for Adam and two for herself. Adam remained mostly quiet during these lectures, though he would nod in agreement whenever Susannah would involve him.

"You must always obey the teacher and get along with the other students, Caleb. That includes sharing and being polite. And absolutely no fighting. Isn't that right, Adam?"

Adam swallowed his whiskey. "Mm hmm," he agreed.

"You're going to be good at school, aren't you, Caleb?" Susannah pressed.

"Yes, Ma," Caleb repeated in a weary voice.

Susannah looked over at Adam to see his lips twitching in a smile. She frowned, not understanding why he was amused. "What's so funny?"

Adam cleared his throat. "Well, you might be close to nagging the boy's ears off. I think he gets the point, darlin'."

"I hope so," she said. "He's never really been around other children before. I worry about him."

"Yes, I was getting that impression," Adam said wryly.

Susannah sank onto her stool. Adam reached out, took her hand, and gave it a squeeze. "You've raised a fine boy. He won't let you down. Just today he helped me collect all the eggs from the coop. He waited patiently for supper. He's a good lad, and he's going to be that way at school too. Aren't you, son?"

Caleb nodded and beamed from ear to ear hearing Adam's words of praise. Susannah smiled at Adam gratefully. He had become much more complimentary of them both ever since Susannah's meltdown over supper.

When Caleb returned from his first day of school with only positive news and excited chatter about the teacher and classmates, she felt relieved, and she began to relax. Her fears were nearly completely gone after a few weeks.

Because her anxiety had subsided, when Caleb was sent home early from school with a black eye, she was taken by surprise. He walked into the cabin just after noon. Dried tears tracked his dirty face, and his lips were pursed in an angry line.

She rushed to him. "Caleb, what happened?" Her heart broke at seeing him hurt, and she quickly made a cold compress for his eye using a strip of old cloth.

Caleb didn't answer her. He held the cloth to his eye and sank onto the floor next to his blocks. He didn't play with them. Instead, he sulked in silence. As time wore on, he remained stubborn in his refusal to talk. No amount of scolding or begging or threatening would compel the boy to tell her what the fight was about. The only information she could wrangle from him was that he'd gotten into a fight with Danny Rogers and the teacher had sent both of them home as a result.

"You know this refusal to talk won't go over too well with your pa, Caleb. You'd better tell him what happened when he gets home, or you're going to be in even worse trouble than you are. This is unacceptable."

"What's unacceptable?" Adam asked from the doorway. He stepped in and closed the door behind him.

Susannah walked to him. Helping him out of his duster, she said, "Caleb got into a fight at school. The teacher sent him home."

Adam's eyebrows shot up. "Oh?" He looked over at Caleb, who was still sitting on the floor, hunched over with the cold compress against his eye. He didn't look up or say hello.

"What the devil happened? Is he all right?" Adam asked.

"He has a bruise around his eye, and I don't know what happened other than the fight was with Danny Rogers. He refuses to tell me anything else." She hung Adam's duster over the hook on the wall. Lowering her voice, she said, "Please don't be too hard on him, Adam. I know he must be punished, but—"

"Hold on," Adam interrupted. "Let's not get ahead of ourselves." He removed his Stetson and tossed it next to his duster, then walked to the sofa and sat down. Susannah remained in place, fretting over whether Adam would be able to get him to talk, and if he did, what the report would be.

"Come here, Caleb," Adam said, his voice so stern that Susannah flinched. Remarkably, all Adam had to do was speak, and the sound of his level voice was far more intimidating than her yelling and scolding.

Caleb placed the strip of damp cloth on the hearth, stood to his feet and trudged over to Adam, his eyes downcast. Adam cupped his chin and turned his face to one side to examine the bruise, then to the other side to make sure he had no other injuries.

"Doesn't look too bad. Why haven't you told your ma what happened?" Adam asked, releasing his chin and pinning him with a stern stare.

"Because I don't want her to know," he explained. The answer was so obvious it would have sounded smart coming from an older child, but coming from

Caleb, it sounded like a sincere attempt at honesty. Susannah could see that he was trying to be brave, but his knees were knocking together and his voice wavered.

"You have to explain better than that, little man," Adam said, his voice gentling. "Are you afraid of punishment?"

Caleb shook his head. "Not from Mama. She doesn't punish me."

The confusion on Adam's face matched how Susannah felt. If he wasn't afraid of punishment, she didn't know why he would refuse to talk.

Adam scratched his beard along his jaw and studied him for a moment before he said, "So you don't want to tell your ma. Is it all right for me to know?"

Caleb lifted his eyes to meet Adam's, and he nodded slowly. Adam glanced over at Susannah. "Give us a minute, darlin'."

She scowled, not understanding her son's reticence to share information with her. "I can't imagine why he would tell you and not me."

"I think I'm about to find out," Adam said, giving her a pointed look that indicated she was to leave the room.

* * *

After Susannah closed the door to their bedroom behind her, Adam turned his attention back to the nervous little boy in front of him.

A rush of memories flooded his mind. He remembered being a boy in Caleb's position, needing to explain to his father how and why he'd gotten into a fight at school. He'd been scared, justifiably so. His father had been as strict as his mother was lenient, and the conversation had ended with his father marching him to the woodshed and tanning his hide.

Caleb was staring down at a button on Adam's shirt. The only sound was the clock ticking away the seconds, which he knew were very long seconds for the boy.

"Look at me," he said, and Caleb obeyed after drawing a deep, shuddering breath.

"Fighting is against the rules, son, but I know sometimes you have to protect yourself. Who hit first, you or the other boy?"

"Me," Caleb said, his lower lip quivering.

Adam closed his eyes briefly, disappointed over the answer. He sighed and said, "Thank you for being honest. It would be worse for you if you'd lied to me, but I must punish you for starting the fight."

"You can punish me, but I'm not sorry I walloped him," Caleb said, jutting out his chin. "Danny said mean words."

"It doesn't matter, son. You can't hit people for talking."

Angry tears flooded his eyes. "But he said the same words about my ma that the shopkeeper said when we were there buying brown sugar, and those words made my mama cry."

That news gave Adam pause, and he felt an ache in his chest as Caleb's comment sank in. Knowing Susannah's reputation in town, he was already fairly certain he knew what Caleb referred to, but to make sure, he asked, "What did Danny Rogers say exactly?"

"That my ma is a two-bit whore." The boy's jaw clenched. "I won't let anyone talk about my ma that way!"

Adam leaned back on the sofa, gathering his thoughts about how to approach the matter. He looked at the little boy standing in front of him, so brave and stubborn in his love for his mother, and his heart swelled with pride. There was no way he could punish him. He scooped Caleb onto his lap and enclosed him in a hug.

"You're not mad at me, Pa?" Caleb asked in a surprised squeak.

"No, son. You defended your ma. A boy has a right to defend his ma, but there are usually better ways of doing it than hitting. If something like this happens again, tell the teacher."

"I will," he promised.

"And tomorrow you and me will go talk to Danny and his pa. I'm just as unhappy as you are, hearing that those words were said about your ma."

Caleb lifted his head and looked into Adam's eyes. "I don't have to say I'm sorry to Danny, do I?"

"Yes, you do. It wasn't right of you to hit him."

Caleb groaned but didn't argue. A moment later, he said, "Pa?"

"Hmm?"

"What's a two-bit whore?"

Adam stifled a chuckle at the innocent question. Clearing his throat, he said, "Well, it's a real nasty way of insulting a woman, saying she's not worth very much. People who say those things don't know your ma like we do. We know she's worth quite a lot, don't we?"

Caleb nodded effusively. "She's the best ma in the whole world. I don't want to tell her what he said about her. It'll make her cry. Don't tell her, please?"

"I'm sorry, little man, but we shouldn't keep her in the dark. She'll be all right, though, just as long as we let her know how special she is to us."

"Maybe I can go pick her some flowers so she feels better?"

"I think that's a fine idea. How about you go ahead and do that while I talk to her?"

"All right," Caleb said, suddenly cheerful. Adam imagined that defending a woman's honor was a heavy burden for a boy to carry alone, especially when he didn't fully understand what that meant.

Adam stared after Caleb, who bounded out the door to fetch flowers. He didn't go to Susannah immediately because he dreaded the conversation he needed to have with her. She would blame herself for Caleb's experience, and it would pain him to see her upset. Still, he felt grateful that he was there to comfort and reassure her.

When he walked to the bedroom, he found her sitting on their bed, fiddling with the lace at her wrists as she was wont to do when nervous. She looked so sweet and fragile that Adam's heart ached. This was who his wife was at the core, underneath her temper and penchant for spoiled behavior—a vulnerable woman who loved with all her heart and who didn't deserve the judgment cast on her by the people in town.

* * *

Susannah met Adam's gaze and saw a look in his eyes that she could only describe as love. Her eyes followed him to where he sat next to her. He wrapped an arm around her shoulders and pulled her to one of her favorite places, up against his chest. Burying her head there, feeling the comfort of his warmth and heartbeat, gave her a sense of calm. No matter what had happened, she knew Adam would make it better.

"What I'm going to say will hurt, darlin', but just think about what a fine job you've done teaching that boy compassion and bravery."

She pulled away slightly so she could look at him. Confused, she said, "This is about the fight?"

He nodded and told her Caleb's story, then said, "He doesn't know what those words mean, and I imagine Danny Rogers is just repeating what he's heard."

She swallowed, trying to keep the lump from rising in her throat. She'd suspected something like this might happen, so it didn't take her completely by surprise. Even though the hostility toward her had faded considerably since she'd married Adam, she still felt cold stares occasionally when she went to town.

"Caleb was intent on defending your honor, and that's all because of you, sweetheart. No matter what anyone tries to say about you, you're raising a boy who respects women, unlike his father who up and left you."

"He's a good boy," she agreed.

"That he is."

"You're wrong about something though," she said with a watery smile. "His father respects women a whole lot."

Adam's face softened into a smile as he took in the meaning of her words. "You're right, I do, but I especially respect you, Susannah."

She quirked her head. "I love hearing you say that, but it's so opposite of what others think about me."

His jaw clenched, and a flash of anger crossed his eyes. "I know. That's why you're worthy of respect. Just hearing what was said about you, well, it makes me so angry I want to tear the town apart. Yet here you are, a generous, kind woman in spite of it all."

Susannah's heart ached with appreciation. "Thank you, Adam. For accepting me, and for everything else. For coming here and running the ranch, for fixing things that need fixing, and for being Caleb's pa. I hope you know how thankful I am for you."

"I do know, honey, and I'm thankful for you too. You showed me what a truly virtuous woman is. She's someone who loves her family and does her best no matter what people say about her. I think folks will come around to seeing you for who you are, but even if they never do, I'll always love and respect you."

Susannah let out a soft sigh of contentment. Tracing a finger around the hard plane of his chest, she gazed into his eyes and said in a teasing voice, wanting to lighten the mood, "Even when I act like a wanton wench in bed?"

Adam coughed a surprised laugh. "Especially then. I love the way you respond to me." To demonstrate, he kissed her until she moaned with desire. He knew how to kiss her in just the right way to fuel her desire—passionately, but not roughly. His tongue teased hers, and his lips latched on and tugged, possessively claiming them as his. She felt small and protected as he wrapped his arms around her and pulled her close.

"Yuck!" Caleb exclaimed from the doorway, interrupting them.

Adam released her lips and loosened his hold on her, and she giggled like a naughty schoolgirl. When she glanced over at Caleb, he was scowling and holding a bouquet of wildflowers with the roots still attached.

"Yuck, is it?" Adam inquired in a serious voice, to which Caleb nodded his head emphatically.

Susannah stopped giggling and composed herself enough to ask, "Are those for me, sweetheart?"

Caleb nodded again but remained in the doorway with the disconcerted frown on his face.

"Well? Come on over and give them to your ma," Adam said.

He wrinkled his nose. "Only if you're done kissing her. *Blech.*"

Adam laughed. "All right, I'm done kissing her for now. I promise."

Caleb gave him a curt nod and walked to Susannah to give her the flowers. He'd no sooner handed them over than Adam grabbed him onto his lap and attacked his cheek with rough kisses while tickling his stomach relentlessly.

"No! Stop!" Caleb screeched, squirming frantically and laughing.

Adam only tortured him for a few seconds before relenting. He held him on his lap with one arm and pulled Susannah close with his other. "You two make me crazy," he said. "Crazy and happy."

Chapter Twelve

The next day, Adam cut his work short and left the range early in the afternoon to ride to town. He arrived at the schoolhouse just after classes had ended and found Caleb sitting on the front steps waiting for him. The bruise around his eye had faded, and he looked to be in good spirits when he ran up to Adam. Without dismounting, Adam leaned over, grasped the boy under his arms, and swung him up to join him in the saddle. Caleb was small enough that Adam settled him in front and held him in place with an arm around his waist.

Reining the horse in the direction of the Rogers' house on Main Street, he asked Caleb if he'd talked to Danny at school that day.

He shook his head. "I don't want to talk to him. He's mean and he's not my friend."

Adam nudged the horse into a faster walk with his heels. "All right, son. You don't have to be friends with him, but you do need to apologize."

Caleb muttered something under his breath, sounding displeased at the reminder.

Adam hoped that Danny's father behaved better than Danny, but he was bracing himself for the worst. A boy tended to mimic his father, and narrow-minded people tended to stay that way.

When they arrived at the Rogers' cottage, Adam and Caleb swung down from the horse. By habit, Adam reached for Caleb's hand, but then decided against taking it. He wanted the boy to feel like he was standing on his own two feet, not being led to apologize.

"Go ahead and knock, Caleb," Adam said, knowing that even doing that was uncomfortable for him. Visiting the Rogers wasn't punishment for fighting, but it was a consequence.

Though Caleb looked near tears, Adam did not comfort him. He felt compassion for the boy, but it was no time for mollycoddling. Caleb rapped on the door and then stuffed his hand into his pocket. "I'm more scared of talking than I was of hitting him," he confessed, his lower lip quivering.

Adam nodded. "I know, son. That's because it's easier for men to fight than to talk things out. But talking is the right way. That's what I want you to learn today."

John Rogers opened the door, and a look of surprise crossed the thin man's face. "Hello," he said to Adam, appearing uncomfortable, and then looked down at Caleb.

"Hello, John," Adam said, and held out his hand, which John shook. "We're wondering if we might have a word with you and Danny. I'm assuming you heard about the fight between our boys?"

He nodded gravely and stepped aside to allow them entrance. They walked into the small entryway, and Caleb stared at the floor. "Say hello to Mr. Rogers, Caleb," Adam admonished.

Caleb mumbled "hello" without looking up, behavior that Adam would have corrected under normal circumstances but allowed to slide this time.

"Danny!" John called. "You've got company."

The boy emerged from another room and trudged over to the small gathering. His lip was swollen and cut where Caleb had slugged him. He stood a few inches taller than Caleb and weighed a fair bit more, but he still appeared small and just as uncomfortable as Caleb in that moment. Placing his hand on Caleb's back in silent encouragement, Adam waited for him to speak.

He glared at Danny with fire in his eyes. "My pa is making me say I'm sorry, so I'm sorry."

"Caleb!" Adam exclaimed sharply. "That's not an apology, young man. Try that again."

His shoulders slouched and he stared down at the floor. "I'm sorry for hitting you," he mumbled.

Adam looked at John. "My boy shouldn't have hit your son. He understands that, but he was defending his ma and he's still angry about what Danny said. I'm angry too, and I'm guessing your boy didn't come up with it on his own."

John shifted on his feet and averted his gaze for a moment before returning to look at Adam, who was giving him a hard stare. "Miss Smith has a reputation around town for being loose. Everyone knows it."

Hearing the gossip spoken aloud gave Adam a new understanding for how Susannah must have felt over the years suffering such condemnation. It filled him with rage. "Her name is Mrs. Harrington now," he said in as calm a voice as he could muster. All of his instincts told him to throttle the lily-livered man standing in front of him, daring to insinuate things about his wife. He drew a deep breath, reminding himself that he needed to set the right example for Caleb. "She's a good wife and a fine mother. But we're not here to convince you of that, only to put this matter to rest so it doesn't happen again." His voice shook with barely controlled anger, and he glared at John, daring him to utter another careless word.

John's eyes widened and he shrank away from Adam ever-so-slightly. "I won't repeat what I said and neither will Danny. She's your wife and I know I would be tetchy if someone said a wrong word about mine."

Adam could see this was as close to an admission of wrongdoing as he would get from John Rogers. It would have to do. He reached down and took Caleb's hand in his. To John, he said, "Thanks for seeing us. We'll be on our way now."

Adam led the boy out the front door. When they reached the horse, Danny came running out. "Hey, Caleb!" he called.

Caleb looked back at him warily, and Adam's hand tightened around his boy's, feeling protective.

"Maybe we could go fishing sometime," Danny said. "You can use my pole if you want, and I'll help you find worms."

Caleb looked from Danny up to Adam and then back at Danny. "That sounds fun," Caleb said tentatively.

Adam felt relieved. He knew this was Danny's way of making amends, and he thought it was well done considering his father's inability to apologize. Smiling, he said, "That's real nice of you, Danny. What do you say, son?" He squeezed Caleb's hand again.

"Thank you." Caleb's response was short, but there was friendliness in his tone.

While riding back, Caleb asked, "How come Danny's pa didn't make him apologize to me?"

The horse clipped along for a few beats before Adam answered. "Every father is different in what he expects from his children. I will always expect you to own up to your mistakes."

Caleb tugged at the horse's mane, seeming to be deep in thought for a while. "Ma says you expect a lot. She says you're hard on her and on me."

"Oh, does she now?" Adam grunted. He was not at all pleased to hear that Susannah was having that discussion with Caleb. *If she thought I was hard on her before…,* he mused to himself wryly. He might just take a strap to her for bellyaching to Caleb. "What else does your ma say?"

"That you're bossy and unbearably strict."

Adam groaned. "Your ma is in so much trouble. What's she thinking, running off her mouth like that to you?"

Caleb shrugged. "I dunno. It doesn't make much sense to me."

"It doesn't? You don't think I'm bossy and strict?"

"You are," Caleb said. "I just don't understand why my ma says those things and then laughs and says how much she loves you. Then after that she cries and says she's crying because she's happy."

Adam laughed heartily at the boy's perspective. "Get used to it. Women don't make a lick of sense sometimes, but life would be awful lonely without them."

* * *

The roast Susannah prepared for supper was delicious, and Adam made sure to compliment her on it, secretly hoping that Martha hadn't been around to assist.

"You really think it's good?" she asked, a broad smile on her face.

"Yup. I reckon it's the best beef I've ever had the pleasure of eating." That was a bit of an exaggeration, but it was worth stretching the truth to see the flush of pleasure it gave his wife.

"I cooked it all on my own. Martha left early today."

He swallowed his bite of food and smiled. "You did a fine job."

Susannah plopped down happily on the stool next to him. "You'll never believe what Martha said to me when she was here."

"What, honey?"

"She asked me to join the cake-baking ladies at the parsonage every Saturday. They want me to be part of the club." Her cheeks were flushed and her eyes sparkled with joy.

Confused, though he was glad to see his wife happy, Adam said, "I thought you hated baking and cooking."

"Yes," she admitted. "But I'm excited because they want to be friends with me."

"I see," Adam said slowly. "They'll be lucky to have you as their friend. You have nothing to prove to those biddies. Don't forget that."

Susannah sidled up to him and sat on his lap. She wrapped her arms around his neck. "I'm lucky to have you as my husband."

"Are you?" he asked in a serious voice. "I hear I am bossy and unbearably strict."

Her eyes widened and her cheeks became pinker. "Oh, well, I didn't mean…" she said haltingly.

Adam kept himself from laughing, but he wasn't able to prevent his eyes from twinkling. When she saw that he was more amused than annoyed, she let out a sigh of relief. "You were the opposite of what I thought I wanted, but you're perfect for me, Adam."

He pulled her close. "I know exactly what you mean because I feel the same way, kitten." They sat in comfortable silence for a spell before Adam broke it by growling in her ear. "Get those dishes washed and meet me in the bedroom. You and I have a matter to settle."

She fairly flew off his lap, looking quite excited by the prospect of engaging in whatever needed settling. When they were alone in their room, Adam tossed her over his lap, shoved down her drawers, and landed a swat on her quivering bare behind. "You're about to find out how bossy I can be, young lady."

She squealed and wriggled enticingly as he brought his hand down again and again in crisp swats.

"Open your legs," he bossed.

She did so, revealing her sex to his view.

"Wider," he growled.

She let out a little whimper as she obeyed, spreading her legs obscenely.

"You're not allowed to move or make noise, no matter what. Got it, kitten?"

She let out a mewl. "What in the heavens are you doing, Adam?"

"I'm being unbearably strict, Susannah," he informed her.

She giggled, which he allowed for only a couple seconds before bringing his hand down on her rump. "Silence begins now. Don't make a peep, and don't move either."

She settled, and he spanked her soundly, catching the inside and backs of her thighs as well as her bottom. She took the swats stoically for some time, though he could tell by her body's clenching that was struggling to absorb the pain. When he continued to spank her mercilessly with no sign of relenting, she eventually yelped, which was what Adam had been waiting for.

He paused. "Did you just make a sound?" A long silence lingered after the question, during which Adam rubbed her hot bottom and watched with amusement as she squirmed. "You disobeyed me, kitten," his voice rumbled softly. "Now I have to punish that naughty cunny of yours."

"What do you— *Arrrrrrghhhh.*" Her words transformed into noncoherent sounds as he clapped his hand over her plump nether lips, spanking her clit and soaking slit. She ground her pussy against his hard leg shamelessly, desperate for relief from both the building pain and the growing pleasure.

"By the way, I agree with you," he said, continuing the spanking on her bottom, then her legs, and then her cunny occasionally, each time making her jump with the shock of it. "I am very, very bossy." He leaned forward and spoke in her ear. "But my little whore needs a bossy man, doesn't she?"

His words caused a shiver and a moan to come from her lips. "Yes," she said breathlessly. "Oh, yes."

He cupped her sex possessively. "Just look at you, spread all over me like a wanton harlot, trying to come. Do you think you deserve to come, little whore?"

"Adam…" she gasped. "I…"

She shuddered and with no further warning arched her back and cried out her release, while Adam fondled her pussy. "Oh, you bad, bad girl," he said dangerously as she settled back over his laps.

"I didn't know," she gasped. "It was a surprise…"

"Bad little whores who come without permission must be dealt with firmly. What should I do with you, kitten?" He stroked her pussy and pinched her highly sensitized clit.

"*Unnghhh*, Adam!" she cried.

He continued to fondle her until he knew by the sounds of her whimpers that her second orgasm was well on its way. "Get on your knees."

HANDLING SUSANNAH

She dropped to the floor in front of him, then gazed at him with wide, adoring eyes. He unbuttoned his trousers, causing his erection to spring forward next to her face. He reached down and twined his fingers in her hair. Closing his hand into a gentle fist, he said. "Take me into your mouth. Show me what a dirty little whore you are."

She opened wide, and Adam nearly lost control as her sweet lips wrapped around his member. "God, Susannah…" he said, closing his eyes. She licked and sucked, taking him deeper and deeper into her mouth. When he opened his eyes, he found her staring at him with a mischievous glint in her eyes.

"You're enjoying this too much," he observed, closing his fist in her hair tighter. "Touch your wet cunt, you bad girl. Seek your own pleasure."

She moaned around his cock and reached between her legs to stroke her sex. As she worked herself into a frenzy, her lips' hold on his cock became looser, driving him crazy. He needed to feel her tight pussy around him.

With a snarl, he lifted her into his arms, laid her on her back and plunged into her drenched opening. He would've come then if he hadn't restrained himself. He didn't want to come right away. He wanted to fuck her, hard, because he could see she wanted to be handled in such a way. He hammered into her, enjoying her gasps and whimpers and enjoying the second loud cry of her orgasm. He held her close to him as she came and then kept her crushed against him as he found his own release moments later.

When the evening turned into night and they were in bed together again, she curled up against him. He caressed her shoulders and rubbed her back, enjoying her sighs and grunts of appreciation. After being so rough with her, it gratified him to be gentle. He loved the task of handling Susannah, and he would always do so with care.

"Goodnight, bossy man," she whispered.

"Goodnight, kitten."

The End

Dear Reader,

Thank you for purchasing *Handling Susannah*. If you enjoyed this book, I invite you to sign up for my newsletter to get future book-release alerts, giveaways, and exclusive excerpts. My newsletter subscribers are the first to know about my book sales and freebies too. Sign up now by visiting my website, ameliasmarts.com.

Amelia Smarts

Books by Amelia Smarts

Mail-Order Grooms Series
Handling Susannah
Catching Betsy
Justice for Elsie

Lost and Found in Thorndale Series
Bringing Trouble Home
When He Returns

Tender Alpha Cowboy Romance
Corralling Callie
Fetching Charlotte Rose
The Unbraiding of Anna Brown

Dominant Daddies
Daddy Takes Charge
Cowboy Daddies: Two Western Romances
His Little Red Lily

Steamy, High-Heat Western Romance
Emma's Surrender
Claimed by the Mountain Man

About Amelia Smarts

Amelia Smarts is a *USA Today* bestselling author who writes kinky romance novels containing domestic discipline, spanking, and Dominance/submission. Usually her stories involve a cowboy, and they always involve a man's firm hand connecting with a woman's naughty backside. Amelia holds graduate and undergraduate degrees in creative writing and English. She loves to read, which allows her writing to be influenced by many different genres in addition to romance, including mystery, adventure, history, and suspense.

Amelia's accolades include:

- Golden Flogger Award Finalist for Best BDSM Book (Emma's Surrender)
- Voted #1 Favorite Historical Romance Author in The Bashful Bookwhore's Poll
- Winner: Best Sweet Spanking Romance (Fetching Charlotte Rose) in the Spanking Romance Reviews Reader's Poll
- Runner-up: Best Historical Western Romance (Claimed by the Mountain Man) in the Spanking Romance Reviews Reader's Poll

To learn more about Amelia and her books, visit ameliasmarts.com.

Made in United States
Orlando, FL
17 June 2024

47991023R00074